NORTH CAROLINA SLAVE NARRATIVES

A Folk History of Slavery in North Carolina
from Interviews with Former Slaves

* * *

Typewritten records prepared by
THE FEDERAL WRITERS' PROJECT
1936-1938

* * *

Published in cooperation with
THE LIBRARY OF CONGRESS

APPLEWOOD BOOKS
Bedford, Massachusetts

The LIBRARY
of CONGRESS

A portion of the proceeds from the sale
of this book is donated to the Library of
Congress, which holds the original Slave
Narratives in its collection.

Thank you for purchasing an Applewood book.
Applewood reprints America's lively classics
--books from the past that are still of
interest to modern readers. For a free copy
of our current catalog, write to:

Applewood Books
P.O. Box 365
Bedford, MA 01730

ISBN 1-55709-020-3

FOREWORD

More than 140 years have elapsed since the ratification of the Thirteenth Amendment to the U.S. Constitution declared slavery illegal in the United States, yet America is still wrestling with the legacy of slavery. One way to examine and understand the legacy of the 19th Century's "peculiar institution" in the 21st century is to read and listen to the stories of those who actually lived as slaves. It is through a close reading of these personal narratives that Americans can widen their understanding of the past, thus enriching the common memory we share.

The American Folklife Center at the Library of Congress is fortunate to hold a powerful and priceless sampling of sound recordings, manuscript interviews, and photographs of former slaves. The recordings of former slaves were made in the 1930s and early 1940s by folklorists John A. and Ruby T. Lomax, Alan Lomax, Zora Neale Hurston, Mary Elizabeth Barnicle, John Henry Faulk, Roscoe Lews, and others. These aural accounts provide the only existing sound of voices from the institution of slavery by individuals who had been held in bondage three generations earlier. These voices can be heard by visiting the web site http://memory.loc.gov/ammem/collections/voices/. Added to the Folklife Center collections, many of the narratives from manuscript sources, which you find in this volume, were collected under the auspices of the United States Works Progress Administration (WPA), and were known as the slave narrative collection. These transcripts are found in the Library of Congress Manuscript Division. Finally, in addition to the Folklife Center photographs, a treasure trove of Farm Security Administration (FSA) photographs (including those of many former slaves) reside in the Prints and Photographs Division here at the nation's library. Together, these primary source materials on audio tape, manuscript and photographic formats are a unique research collection for all who would wish to study and understand the emotions, nightmares, dreams, and determination of former slaves in the United States.

The slave narrative sound recordings, manuscript materials, and photographs are invaluable as windows through which we can observe and be touched by the experiences of slaves who lived in the mid-19th century. At the same time, these archival materials are the fruits of an extraordinary documentary effort of the 1930s. The federal government, as part of its response to the Great Depression, organized unprecedented national initiatives to document the lives, experiences, and cultural traditions of ordinary Americans. The slave narratives, as documents of the Federal Writers Project, established and delineated our modern concept of "oral history." Oral history, made possible by the advent of sound recording technology, was "invented" by folklorists, writers, and other cultural documentarians under the aegis of the Library of Congress and various WPA offices—especially the Federal Writers' project—during the 1930s. Oral history has subsequently become both a new tool for the discipline of history, and a new cultural pastime undertaken in homes, schools, and communities by Americans of all walks of life. The slave narratives you read in the pages that follow stand as our first national exploration of the idea of oral history, and the first time that ordinary Americans were made part of the historical record.

The American Folklife Center has expanded upon the WPA tradition by continuing to collect oral histories from ordinary Americans. Contemporary projects such as our Veterans History Project, StoryCorps Project, Voices of Civil Rights Project, as well as our work to capture the stories of Americans after September 11, 2001 and of the survivors of Hurricanes Katrina and Rita, are all adding to the Library of Congress holdings that will enrich the history books of the future. They are the oral histories of the 21st century.

Frederick Douglas once asked: can "the white and colored people of this country be blended into a common nationality, and enjoy together...under the same flag, the inestimable blessings of life, liberty, and the pursuit of happiness, as neighborly citizens of a common country? I believe they can." We hope that the words of the former slaves in these editions from Applewood Books will help Americans achieve Frederick Douglas's vision of America by enlarging our understanding of the legacy of slavery in all of our lives. At the same time, we in the American Folklife Center and the Library of Congress hope these books will help readers understand the importance of oral history in documenting American life and culture—giving a voice to all as we create our common history.

Peggy A. Bulger

Peggy Bulger
Director, The American Folklife Center
Library of Congress

A NOTE FROM THE PUBLISHER

Since 1976, Applewood Books has been republishing books from America's past. Our mission is to build a picture of America through its primary sources. The book you hold in your hand is a testament to that mission. Published in cooperation with the Library of Congress, this collection of slave narratives is reproduced exactly as writers in the Works Progress Administration's Federal Writers' Project (1936–1938) originally typed them.

As publishers, we thought about how to present these documents. Rather than making them more readable by resetting the type, we felt that there was more value in presenting the narratives in their original form. We believe that to fully understand any primary source, one must understand the period of time in which the source was written or recorded. Collected seventy years after the emancipation of American slaves, these narratives had been preserved by the Library of Congress, fortunately, as they were originally created. In 1941, the Library of Congress microfilmed the typewritten pages on which the narratives were originally recorded. In 2001, the Library of Congress digitized the microfilm and made the narratives available on their American Memory web site. From these pages we have reproduced the original documents, including both the marks of the writers of the time and the inconsistencies of the type. Some pages were missing or completely illegible, and we have used a simple typescript provided by the Library of Congress so that the page can be read. Although the font occasionally can make these narratives difficult to read, we believe that it is important not only to preserve the narratives of the slaves but also to preserve the documents themselves, thereby commemorating the groundbreaking effort that produced them. That way, also, we can give you, the reader, not only a collection of the life stories of ex-slaves, but also a glimpse into the time in which these stories were collected, the 1930s.

These are powerful stories by those who lived through slavery. No institution was more divisive in American history than slavery. From the very founding of America and to the present day, slavery has touched us all. We hope these real stories of real lives are preserved for generations of Americans to come.

Please note: This volume is not the complete collection of narratives that were recorded for this state. The additional parts are available in additional volumes from Applewood Books. For the purposes of listing the narratives included in this book, we have provided the original typewritten contents page and placed a box around the narratives included in this volume.

INFORMANTS

N. C. District_No. 2_   Subject __Louisa Adams_____

Worker T. Pat Matthews   Person Interviewed _Louisa Adams

No. Words__1384____   Editor_Daisy Bailey Waitt_____

LOUISA ADAMS

"My name is Louisa Adams. I wuz bawned in Rockingham, Richmond County, North Carolina. I wuz eight years old when the Yankees come through. I belonged to Marster Tom A. Covington, Sir. My mother wuz named Easter, and my father wuz named Jacob. We were all Covingtons. No Sir, I don't know whur my mother and father come from. Soloman wuz brother number one, then Luke, Josh, Stephen, Asbury. My sisters were Jane, Frances, Wincy, and I wuz nex'. I 'members grandmother. She wuz named Lovie Wall. They brought her here from same place. My aunts were named, one wuz named Nicey, and one wuz named Jane. I picked feed for the white folks. They sent many of the chillun to work at the salt mines, where we went to git salt. My brother Soloman wuz sent to the salt mines. Luke looked atter the sheep. He knocked down china berries for 'em. (Dad and mammie had their own gardens and hogs. We were compelled to walk about at night to live. We were so hongry we were bound to steal or parish. This trait seems to be handed down from slavery days. Sometimes I thinks dis might be so.) Our food wuz bad. Marster worked us hard and gave us nuthin. We had to use what we made in the garden to eat. We also et our hogs. Our clothes were

bad, and beds were sorry. (We went barefooted in a way.
What I mean by that is, that we had shoes part of the time.
We got one pair o' shoes a year. When dey wored out we
went barefooted. Sometimes we tied them up with strings,
and they were so ragged de tracks looked like bird tracks,
where we walked in the road. We lived in log houses daubed
with mud. They called 'em the slaves houses. My old daddy
partly raised his chilluns on game. He caught rabbits,
coons, an' possums. He would work all day and hunt at night.
We had no holidays. They did not give us any fun as I know.
I could eat anything I could git. I tell you de truth,
slave time wuz slave time wid us. My brother wore his
shoes out, and had none all thu winter. His feet cracked
open and bled so bad you could track him by the blood. When
the Yankees come through, he got shoes.

"I wuz married in Rockingham. I don't 'member when.
Mr. Jimmie Covington, a preacher, a white man, married us.
I married James Adams who lived on a plantation near Rockingham. I had a nice blue wedding dress. My husband wuz
dressed in kinder light clothes, best I rickerlect. It's
been a good long time, since den tho'.

"I sho do 'member my Marster Tom Covington and his wife
too, Emma. De old man wuz the very Hick. He would take
what we made and lowance us, dat is lowance it out to my

daddy after he had made it. My father went to Steven
Covington, Marster Tom's brother, and told him about it,
and his brother Stephen made him gib father his meat back
to us.

"My missus wuz kind to me, but Mars. Tom wuz the buger.
It wuz a mighty bit plantation. I don't know how many
slaves wuz on it, there were a lot of dem do'. Dere were
overseers two of 'em. One wuz named Bob Covington and the
other Charles Covington. They were colored men. I rode
with them. I rode wid 'em in the carriage sometimes. De
carriage had seats dat folded up. Bob wuz overseer in de
field, and Charles wuz carriage driver. All de plantation
wuz fenced in, dat is all de fields, wid rails; de rails
wuz ten feet long. We drawed water wid a sweep and pail.
De well wuz in the yard. De mules for the slaves wuz in
town, dere were none on the plantation. Dey had 'em in
town; dey waked us time de chicken crowed, and we went to
work just as soon as we could see how to make a lick wid
a hoe.

"Lawd, you better not be caught wid a book in yor han'.
If you did, you were sold. Dey didn't 'low dat. I kin
read a little, but I can't write. I went to school after
slavery and learned to read. We didn't go to school but
three or four week a year, and learned to read.

"Dere wuz no church on the plantation, and we were

not lowed to have prayer meetings. No parties, no candy
pullings, nor dances, no sir, not a bit. I 'member goin'
one time to the white folkses church, no baptizing dat
I 'member. Lawd have mercy, ha! ha! No. De pateroller
were on de place at night. You couldn't travel without
a pas.

"We got few possums. I have greased my daddy's back
after he had been whupped until his back wuz cut to pieces.
He had to work jis the same. When we went to our houses
at night, we cooked our suppers at night, et, and then
went to bed. If fire wuz out or any work needed doin'
around de house we had to work on Sundays. They did not
gib us Christmas or any other holidays. We had corn shuckings. I herd 'em talkin' of cuttin de corn pile right square
in two. One wud git on one side, another on the other side
and see which out beat. They had brandy at the corn shuckin'
and I herd Sam talkin' about gittin' drunk.

"I 'member one 'oman dying. Her name wuz Caroline Covington. I didn't go to the grave. But you know they had a
little cart used with hosses to carry her to the grave, jist
a one horse wagon, jist slipped her in there.

"Yes, I 'member a field song. It wuz 'Oh! come let us go
where pleasure never dies. Great fountain gone over'. Dats
one uv 'em. We had a good doctor when we got sick. He come

to see us. The slaves took herbs. dey found in de woods.
Dat's what I do now, Sir. I got some 'erbs right in my
kitchen now.

"When the Yankees come through I did not know anything
about 'em till they got there. Jist like they were poppin
up out of de ground. One of the slaves wuz at his master's
house you know, and he said, 'The Yankees are in Cheraw,
and the Yankees are in town'. It didn't sturb me at
tall. I wuz not afraid of de Yankees. I 'member dey went
to Miss Emma's house, and went in de smoke house and emptied
every barrel of lasses right in de floor and scattered de
cracklings on de floor. I went dere and got some of 'em.
Miss Emma wuz my missus. Dey just killed de chickans, hogs
too, and old Jeff the dog; they shot him through the thoat.
I 'member how his mouth flew open when dey shot him. One
uv 'em went into de tater bank, and we chillun wanted to go
out dere. Mother wouldn't let us. She wuz fraid uv 'em.

"Abraham Lincoln freed us by the help of the Lawd, by
his help. Slavery wuz owin to who you were with. If you
were with some one who wuz good and had some feelin's for
you it did tolerable well; yea, tollerable well.

"We left the plantation soon as de surrender. We lef'
right off. We went to goin' towards Fayetteville, North
Carolina. We climbed over fences and were just broke down

chillun, feet sore. We had a little meat, corn meal, a tray,
and mammy had a tin pan. One night we came to a old house;
some one had put wheat straw in it. We staid there, next
mornin', we come back home. Not to Marster's, but to a white
'oman named Peggy McClinton, on her plantation. We stayed
there a long time. De Yankees took everything dey could, but
dey didn't give us anything to eat. Dey give some of de
'omen shoes.

"I thinks Mr. Roosevelt is a fine man and he do all he
can for us.

District No_____3_____   Title___Ida Adkins Ex-slave___

Worker___Travis Jordan____   Interviewed___Ida Adkins_____

No. Words___1500_____   County Home, Durham, N.C.____

IDA ADKINS

Ex-slave 79 years.

"I was born befo' de war. I was about eight years ole when de Yankee mens come through.

My mammy an' pappy, Hattie an' Jim Jeffries belonged to Marse Frank Jeffries. Marse Frank come from Mississippi, but when I was born he an' Mis' Mary Jane was livin' down here near Louisburg in North Carolina whare dey had er big plantation an' I don't know how many niggers. Marse Frank was good to his niggers, 'cept that he never give dem enough to eat. He worked dem hard on half rations, but he didn' believe in all de time beatin' an' sellin' dem.

My pappy worked at de stables, he was er good hossman, but my mammy worked at de big house helpin' Mis' Mary Jane. Mammy worked in de weavin' room. I can see her now settin' at de weavin' machine an' hear de pedals goin' plop, plop, as she treaded dem wid her feets. She was a good weaver. I stayed 'roun' de big house too, pickin' up chips, sweepin' de yard an' such as dat. Mis' Mary Jane was quick as er whip-po'-will. She had black eyes dat snapped, an' dey seed everythin'. She could turn her head so quick dat she'd ketch you every time you tried to steal a lump of sugar. I liked Marse Frank better den I did Mis' Mary Jane. All us little chillun called him Big Pappy. Every time he come back he brung us niggers back some candy. (He went to Raleigh erbout twice er year.) Raleigh wuz er far ways from de plantation—near 'bout sixty miles. It always took Marse Frank three days to make de trip. A day to go, er day to stay in town, an' a day to come back. Den he always got home in de night. Ceptn' when he rode ho'se back 'stead of de carriage, den sometimes he got home by sun down.

Marse Frank didn' go to de war. He was too ole. So when de Yankees come through dey foun' him at home. When Marse Frank seed de blue coats comin' down de road he run an' got his gun. De Yankees was on horses. I ain't never seed so many men. Dey was thick as hornets comin' down de road in a cloud of dust. Dey come up to de house an' tied de horses to de palin's; dey wuz so many dey 'roun' de yard. When dey seed Marse Frank standin' on de porch wid de gun leveled on dem, dey got mad. Time Marse Frank done shot a bully Yankee snatched de gun away an' tole Marse Frank to hold up his hands. Den dey tied his hands an' pushed him down on de floor 'side de house an' tole him dat if he moved a inch dey would shoot him. Den dey went in de house.

I was skeered near 'bout to death, but I run in de kitchen an' got a butcher knife, an' when de Yankees wasn't lookin', I tried to cut de rope an' set Marse Frank free. But one of dem blue debils seed me an' come runnin'. He say:

'Whut you doin', you black brat, you stinkin' little alligator bait!' He snatched de knife from my hand an' told me to stick out my tongue, dat he was gwine to cut it off. I let out a yell an' run behind de house.

Some of de Yankees was in de smoke house gettin' de meat, some

of dem was at de stables gettin' de horses, an' some of dem was
in de house gettin' de silver an' things. I seed dem put de big
silver pitcher an' tea pot in a bag. Den dey took de knives an'
fo'ks an' all de candle sticks an' platters off de side board.
Dey went in de parlor an' got de gold clock dat was Mis' Mary Jane's
gran'mammy's. Den dey got all de jewelry out of Mis' Mary Jane's
box. Dey went up to Mis' Mary Jane, an' while she looked at
dem wid her black eyes snappin', dey took de rings off her fingers;
den dey took her gold bracelet; dey even took de ruby ear rings out
of her ears an' de gold comb out of her hair.

I done quit peepin' in de window an' was standin' 'side de house
when de Yankees come out in de yard wid all de stuff dey was totin'
off. Marse Frank was still settin' on de porch floor wid his hands
tied an' couldn' do nothin'. 'Bout dat time I seed de bee gums in
de side yard. Dey was a whole line of gums. Little as I was I had
a notion. I run an' got me a long stick an' turned over every
one of dem gums. Den I stirred dem bees up wid dat stick till dey
was so mad I could smell de pizen. An' bees! you ain't never seed
de like of bees. Dey was swarmin' all over de place. Dey sailed into
dem Yankees like bullets, each one madder den de other. Dey lit on
dem horses till dey looked like dey wuz alive wid varmints. De
horses broke dey bridles an' tore down de palin's an' lit out down
de road. But dat runnin' wuzn' nothin' to what dem Yankees done. Dey
bust out cussin', but what did a bee keer about cuss words! Dey

lit on dem blue coats an' every time dey lit dey stuck in a pizen sting.   De Yankee's forgot all a'bout de meat an' things dey done stole; dey took off down de road on a run, passin' de horses. De bees was right after dem in a long line. Dey'd zoom an' zip, an' zoom an' zip, an' every time dey'd zip a Yankee would yell.

When dey'd gone Mis' Mary Jane untied Marse Frank. Den dey took all de silver, meat an' things de Yankees lef' behin' an' buried it so if dey come back dey couldn' fin' it. ¶Den dey called ma an' said:

'Ida Lee, if you hadn't turned over dem bee gums de Yankees would have toted off near 'bout everythin' fine we got. We want to give you somethin' you can keep so' you'll always remember dis day, an' how you run de Yankees away.'

Den Mis' Mary Jane took a plain gold ring off her finger an' put it on mine. An' I been wearin' it ever since.

N. C. District No. 2   Subject Ex-Slave Story

Worker Mary A. Hicks   Person Interviewed Martha Allen

No. Words   402   Editor Daisy Bailey Waitt

EX-SLAVE STORY

An interview with Martha Allen, 78, of 1318 South Person
Street, Raleigh.

"I wuz borned in Craven County seventy eight years
ago. My pappa wuz named Andrew Bryant an' my mammy wuz
named Harriet. My brothers wuz John Franklin, Alfred, an'
Andrew. I ain't had no sisters. I reckon dat we is what
yo' call a general mixture case I am part Injun, part white,
an' part nigger.

"My mammy belonged ter Tom Edward Gaskin an' she
wuzn't half fed. De cook nussed de babies while she cooked,
so dat de mammies could wuck in de fiel's, an' all de mammies
done wuz stick de babies in at de kitchen do' on dere way
ter de fiel's. I'se hyard mammy say dat dey went ter wuck
widout breakfast, an' dat when she put her baby in de kitchen
she'd go by de slop bucket an' drink de slops from a long
handled goard.

"De slave driver wuz bad as he could be, an' de slaves
got awful beatin's.

"De young marster sorta wanted my mammy, but she tells
him no, so he chunks a lightwood knot an' hits her on de haid
wid it. Dese white mens what had babies by nigger wimmens
wuz called 'Carpet Gitters'. My father's father wuz one o'
dem.

"Yes mam, I'se mixed plenty case my mammy's grandmaw
wuz Cherokee Injun.

"I doan know nothin' 'bout no war, case marster carried
us ter Cedar Falls, near Durham an' dar's whar we come free;

"I 'members dat de Ku Klux uster go ter de Free
Issues houses, strip all de family an' whup de ole folkses.
Den dey dances wid de pretty yaller gals an' goes ter bed
wid dem. Dat's what de Ku Klux wuz, a bunch of mean mens
tryin' ter hab a good time.)

"I'se wucked purty hard durin' my life an' I done
my courtin' on a steer an' cart haulin' wood ter town ter
sell. He wuz haulin' wood too on his wagin, an' he'd beat
me ter town so's dat he could help me off'n de wagin. I
reckon dat dat wuz as good a way as any.

"I tries ter be a good christian but I'se got dis-
gusted wid dese young upstart niggers what dances in de
chu'ch. Dey says dat dey am truckin' an' dat de Bible ain't
forbid hit, but I reckin dat I knows dancin' whar I sees hit."

N. C. District __II__   Subject __Story of Joseph__

Worker __Mrs. Edith S. Hibbs__   __Anderson__

No. Words __275__   Interviewed __Joseph Anderson__

Edited __Mrs. W. N. Harriss__   __1113 Rankin St.,Wilmington,N.C__

A large frame building was built over it. At the top of the
earth there was an entrance door and steps leading down to the
bottom of the hole. Other things besides ice were stored there.
There was a still on the plantation and barrels of brandy were
stored in the ice house, also pickles, preserves and cider.)

"Many of the things we used were made on the place. There
was a grist mill, tannery, shoe shop, blacksmith shop, and looms
for weaving cloth.

"There were about one hundred and sixty-two slaves on the
plantation and every Sunday morning all the children had to be
bathed, dressed, and their hair combed and carried down to
marster's for breakfast. It was a rule that all the little
colored children eat at the great house every Sunday morning
in order that marster and missus could watch them eat so they
could know which ones were sickly and have them doctored.

"The slave children all carried a mussel shell in their
hands to eat with. The food was put on large trays and the
children all gathered around and ate, dipping up their food
with their mussel shells which they used for spoons. Those
who refused to eat or those who were ailing in any way had to
come back to the great house for their meals and medicine
until they were well.

"Marster had a large apple orchard in the Tar River low
grounds and up on higher ground and nearer the plantation house
there was on one side of the road a large plum orchard and on
the other side was an orchard of peaches, cherries, quinces and

grapes. We picked the quinces in August and used them for
preserving. Marster and missus believed in giving the slaves
plenty of fruit, especially the children.

"Marster had three children, one boy named Dallas, and
two girls, Bettie and Carrie. He would not allow slave
children to call his children marster and missus unless the
slave said little marster or little missus. He had four white
overseers but they were not allowed to whip a slave. If there
was any whipping to be done he always said he would do it. He
didn't believe in whipping so when a slave got so bad he could
not manage him he sold him.

"Marster didn't quarrel with anybody, missus would not
speak short to a slave, but both missus and marster taught
slaves to be obedient in a nice quiet way. The slaves were
taught to take their hats and bonnets off before going into the
house, and to bow and say, 'Good morning Marster Sam and Missus
Evaline'. Some of the little negroes would go down to the great
house and ask them when it wus going to rain, and when marster
or missus walked in the grove the little Negroes would follow
along after them like a gang of kiddies. Some of the slave
children wanted to stay with them at the great house all the
time. They knew no better of course and seemed to love marster
and missus as much as they did their own mother and father.
Marster and missus always used gentle means to get the children
out of their way when they bothered them and the way the
children loved and trusted them wus a beautiful sight to see.

"Patterollers were not allowed on the place unless they came peacefully and I never knew of them whipping any slaves on marster's place. Slaves were carried off on two horse wagons to be sold. I have seen several loads leave. They were the unruly ones. Sometimes he would bring back slaves, once he brought back two boys and three girls from the slave market.

"Sunday wus a great day on the plantation. Everybody got biscuits Sundays. The slave women went down to marsters for their Sunday allowance of flour. All the children ate break-fast at the great house and marster and missus gave out fruit to all. The slaves looked forward to Sunday as they labored through the week. It was a great day. Slaves received good treatment from marster and all his family.

"We were allowed to have prayer meetings in our homes and we also went to the white folks church.

"They would not teach any of us to read and write. Books and papers were forbidden. Marster's children and the slave children played together. I went around with the baby girl Carrie to other plantations visiting. She taught me how to talk low and how to act in company. My association with white folks and my training while I was a slave is why I talk like white folks.

"Bettie Brodie married a Dr. Webb from Boylan, Virginia. Carrie married a Mr. Joe Green of Franklin County. He was a big southern planter.

"The war was begun and there were stories of fights and freedom. The news went from plantation to plantation and while the slaves acted natural and some even more polite than usual, they prayed for freedom. Then one day I heard something that sounded like thunder and missus and marster began to walk around and act queer. The grown slaves were whispering to each other. Sometimes they gathered in little gangs in the grove. Next day I heard it again, boom, boom, boom. I went and asked missus 'is it going to rain?' She said, 'Mary go to the ice house and bring me some pickles and preserves.' I went and got them. She ate a little and gave me some. Then she said, 'You run along and play.' In a day or two everybody on the plantation seemed to be disturbed and marster and missus were crying. Marster ordered all the slaves to come to the great house at nine o'clock. Nobody was working and slaves were walking over the grove in every direction. At nine o'clock all the slaves gathered at the great house and marster and missus came out on the porch and stood side by side. You could hear a pin drap everything was so quiet. Then marster said, 'Good morning,' and missus said, 'Good morning, children'. They were both crying. Then marster said, 'Men, women and children, your are free. You are no longer my slaves. The Yankees will soon be here.'

"Marster and missus then went into the house got two large arm chairs put them on the porch facing the avenue and sat down side by side and remained there watching.

In about an hour there was one of the blackest clouds coming
up the avenue from the main road. It was the Yankee soldiers,
they finally filled the mile long avenue reaching from marster's
house to the main Louisburg road and spread out over the mile
square grove. The mounted men dismounted. The footmen stacked
their shining guns and began to build fires and cook. They
called the slaves, saying, 'Your are free.' Slaves were whooping
and laughing and acting like they were crazy. Yankee soldiers
were shaking hands with the Negroes and calling them Sam, Dinah,
Sarah and asking them questions. They busted the door to the
smoke house and got all the hams. They went to the icehouse and
got several barrels of brandy, and such a time. The Negroes and
Yankees were cooking and eating together. The Yankees told them
to come on and join them, they were free. Marster and missus
sat on the porch and they were so humble no Yankee bothered
anything in the great house. The slaves were awfully excited.
The Yankees stayed there, cooked, eat, drank and played music
until about night, then a bugle began to blow and you never saw
such getting on horses and lining up in your life. In a few
minutes they began to march, leaving the grove which was soon
as silent as a grave yard. They took marster's horses and cattle
with them and joined the main army and camped just across
Cypress Creek one and one half miles from my marster's place
on the Louisburg Road.

"When they left the country, lot of the slaves want with
them and soon there were none of marster's slaves left. They
wondered around for a year from place to place, fed and working

most of the time at some other slave owner's plantation and getting more homesick every day.

"The second year after the surrender our marster and missus got on their carriage and went and looked up all the Negroes they heard of who ever belonged to them. Some who went off with the Yankees were never heard of again. When marster and missus found any of theirs they would say, 'Well, come on back home,' My father and mother, two uncles and their families moved back. Also Lorenza Brodie, and John Brodie and their families moved back. Several of the young men and women who once belonged to him came back. Some were so glad to get back they cried, 'cause fare had been mighty bad part of the time they were rambling around and they were hungry. When they got back marster would say, 'Well you have come back home have you, and the Negroes would say, 'Yes marster.' Most all spoke of them as missus and marster as they did before the surrender, and getting back home was the greatest pleasure of all.

"We stayed with marster and missus and went to their church, the Maple Springs Baptist church, until they died.

"Since the surrender I married James Anderson. I had four children, one boy and three girls.

"I think slavery was a mighty good thing for mother, father, me and the other members of the family, and I cannot say anything but good for my old marster and missus, but I can only speak for those whose conditions I have known during slavery and since. For myself and them, I will say again, slavery was a mighty good thing."

N. C. District <u>No. 2</u>　　　Subject <u>Cornelia Andrews</u>

Worker <u>Mary A. Hicks</u>　　　Story teller <u>Cornelia Andrews</u>

No. Words <u>789</u>　　　Editor <u>Daisy Bailey Waitt</u>

CORNELIA ANDREWS

An interview on May 21, 1937 with Cornelia Andrews of
Smithfield, Johnston County, who is 87 years old.

"De fust marster dat I 'members wuz Mr. Cute
Williams an' he wuz a good marster, but me an' my mammy
an' some of de rest of 'em wuz sold to Doctor McKay Vaden
who wuz not good ter us.

"Doctor Vaden owned a good-sized plantation, but
he had just eight slaves. We had plank houses, but we
ain't had much food an' clothes. We wored shoes wid wooden
bottom in de winter an' no shoes in de summer. We ain't
had much fun, nothin' but candy pullin's 'bout onct a year.
We ain't raised no cane but marster buyed one barrel of
'lasses fer candy eber year.

"Yo' know dat dar wuz a big slave market in
Smithfield dem days, dar wuz also a jail, an' a whippin'
post. I 'members a man named Rough somethin' or other,
what bought forty er fifty slaves at de time an' carried
'em ter Richmond to re-sell. He had four big black horses
hooked ter a cart, an' behind dis cart he chained de slaves,
an' dey had ter walk, or trot all de way ter Richmond. De
little ones Mr. Rough would throw up in de cart an' off

dey'd go no'th. Dey said dat der wuz one day at Smithfield
dat three hundret slaves wuz sold on de block. Dey said
dat peoples came from fer an' near, eben from New Orleans
ter dem slave sales. Dey said dat way 'fore I wuz borned
dey uster strip dem niggers start naked an' gallop 'em
ober de square so dat de buyers could see dat dey warn't
scared nor deformed.

"While I could 'member dey'd sell de mammies 'way
from de babies, an' dere wuzn't no cryin' 'bout it whar
de marster would know 'bout it nother. Why? Well, dey'd
git beat black an' blue, dat's why.

"Wuz I eber beat bad? No mam, I wuzn't."

(Here the daughter, a graduate of Cornell University,
who was in the room listening came forward. "Open your
shirt, mammy, and let the lady judge for herself." The old
ladies eyes flashed as she sat bolt upright. She seemed
ashamed, but the daughter took the shirt off, exposing the
back and shoulders which were marked as though branded with
a plaited cowhide whip. There was no doubt of that at all.)

"I wuz whupped public", she said tonelessly, "for
breaking dishes an' 'bein' slow. I wuz at Mis' Carrington's
den, an' it wuz jist 'fore de close o' de war. I wuz in

de kitchen washin' dishes an' I draps one. De missus calls
Mr. Blount King, a patteroller, an' he puts de whuppin' yo'
sees de marks of on me. My ole missus foun' it out an' she
comed an' got me."

A friend of the interviewer who was present remarked,
"That must have been horrible to say the least."

"Yo' doan know nothin," the old Negro blazed. "Alex
Heath, a slave wuz beat ter death, hyar in Smithfield. He
had stold something, dey tells me, anyhow he wuz sentenced
ter be put ter death, an' de folkses dar in charge 'cided
ter beat him ter death. Dey gib him a hundret lashes fer
nine mornin's an' on de ninth mornin' he died.

"My uncle Daniel Sanders, wuz beat till he wuz cut
inter gashes an' he wuz tu be beat ter death lak Alex wuz,
but one day atter dey had beat him an' throwed him back in
jail wid out a shirt he broke out an' runned away. He went
doun in de riber swamp an' de blow flies blowed de gashes
an' he wuz unconscious when a white man found him an' tuk
him home wid him. He died two or three months atter dat
but he neber could git his body straight ner walk widout
a stick; he jist could drag.

"I 'specks dat I doan know who my pappy wuz, maybe
de stock nigger on de plantation. My pappy an' mammy jist

stepped ober de broom an' course I doan know when. Yo'
knows dey ain't let no little runty nigger have no chilluns.
Naw sir, dey ain't, dey operate on dem lak dey does de male
hog so's dat dey can't have no little runty chilluns.

"Some of de marsters wuz good an' some of dem wuz
bad. I wuz glad ter be free an' I lef' der minute I finds
out dat I is free. I ain't got no kick a-comin' not none
at all. Some of de white folkses wuz slaves, ter git ter
de United States an' we niggers ain't no better, I reckons."

N.C. District   No. 2   Subject: A SLAVE STORY
                             (Princess Quango Henna-
donah Perceriah).

No. Words   22,289   Reference: MARY ANNGADY

Worker: T. Pat Matthews   Editor: George L. Andrews

MARY ANNGADY

(Princess Quango Hennadonah Perceriah)
1110 Oakwood Avenue, Raleigh, North Carolina.

"I was eighteen years old in 1875 but I wanted to get married so I gave my age as nineteen. I wish I could re-call some of the ole days when I was with my missus in Orange County, playing with my brothers and other slave children.

"I was owned by Mr. Franklin Davis and my madam was Mrs. Bettie Davis. I and my brother used to scratch her feet and rub them for her; you know how old folks like to have their feet rubbed. My brother and I used to scrap over who should scratch and rub her feet. She would laugh and tell us not to do that way that she loved us both. Sometimes she let me sleep at her feet at night. She was plenty good to all of the slaves. Her daughter Sallie taught me my A B C's in Webster's Blue Back spelling Book. When I learned to Spell B-a-k-e-r, Baker, I thought that was something. The next word I felt proud to spell was s-h-a-d-y, shady, the next l-a-d-y, lady. I would spell them out loud as I picked up chips in the yard to build a fire with. My missus Bettie gave me a blue back spelling book.

"My father was named James Mason and he belonged to
James Mason of Chapel Hill. Mother and I and my four
brothers belonged to the same man and we also lived in the
town. I never lived on a farm or plantation in my life.
I know nothing about farming. All my people are dead and
I cannot locate any of marster's family if they are living.
Marster's family consisted of two boys and two girls- Willie,
Frank, Lucy and Sallie. Marster was a merchant, selling
general merchandise. I remember eating a lot of brown
sugar and candy at his store.

"My mother was a cook. They allowed us a lot of
privileges and it was just one large happy family with
plenty to eat and wear, good sleeping places and nothing
to worry about. They were of the Presbyterian faith and
we slaves attended Sunday school and services at their
church. There were about twelve slaves on the lot. The
houses for slaves were built just a little ways back from
marster's house on the same lot. The Negro and white
children played together, and there was little if any
difference made in the treatment given a slave child and
a white child. I have religious books they gave me.
Besides the books they taught me, they drilled me in
etiquette of the times and also in courtesy and respect
to my superiors until it became a habit and it was perfectly
natural for me to be polite.

"The first I knew of the Yankees was when I was out
in my marster's yard picking up chips and they came along,
took my little brother and put him on a horse's back and
carried him up town. I ran and told my mother about it.
They rode brother over the town a while, having fun out of
him, then they brought him back. Brother said he had a
good ride and was pleased with the blue jackets as the
Yankee soldiers were called.

"We had all the silver and valuables hid and the
Yankees did not find them, but they went into marster's
store and took what they wanted. They gave my father a
box of hardtack and a lot of meat. Father was a Christian
and he quoted one of the Commandments when they gave him
things they had stolen from others. 'Thou shalt not steal',
quoth he, and he said he did not appreciate having stolen
goods given to him.

"I traveled with the white folks in both sections
of the country, north and south, after the War Between the
States. I kept traveling with them and also continued
my education. They taught me to recite and I made money
by reciting on many of the trips. Since the surrender I
have traveled in the north for various Charitable Negro
Societies and Institutions and people seemed very much
interested in the recitation I recited called "When Malinda
Sings".

"The first school I attended was after the war closed.
The school was located in Chapel Hill, North Carolina, and
was taught by a Yankee white woman from Philadelphia. We
remained in Chapel Hill only a few years after the war
ended when we all moved to Raleigh, and I have made it my
home ever since. I got the major part of my education in
Raleigh under Dr. H.M. Tupper* who taught in the second
Baptist Church, located on Blount Street. Miss Mary Lathrop,
a colored teacher from Philadelphia, was an assistant teacher
in Dr. Tupper's School. I went from there to Shaw
Collegiate Institute, which is now Shaw University.

"I married Aaron Stallings of Warrenton, North Carolina
while at Shaw. He died and I married Rev. Matthews Anngady
of Monrovia, west coast of Africa, Liberia, Pastor of First
Church. I helped him in his work here, kept studying the
works of different authors, and lecturing and reciting.
My husband, the Rev. Matthews Anngady, died and I gave a lot of
my time to the cause of Charity, and while on a lecture
tour of Massachusetts in the interest of this feature of
colored welfare for Richmond, Va., the most colorful incident
of my eventful life happened when I met Quango Hennadonah
Perceriah, an Abyssinian Prince, who was traveling and
lecturing on the customs of his country and the habits of
its people. Our mutual interests caused our friendship
to ripen fast and when the time of parting came, when each

of us had finished our work in Massachusetts, he going back
to his home in New York City and I returning to Richmond, he
asked me to correspond with him. I promised to do so and
our friendship after a year's correspondence became love and
he proposed and I accepted him. We were married in Raleigh
by Rev. J.J. Worlds, pastor of the First Baptist Church,
colored.

"P.T. Barnum had captured my husband when he was a
boy and brought him to America from Abyssinia, educated him
and then sent him back to his native country. He would not
stay and soon he was in America again. He was of the Catholic
faith in America and they conferred the honor of priesthood
upon him but after he married me this priesthood was taken
away and he joined the Episcopal Church. After we were
married we decided to go on an extensive lecture tour. He
had been a headsman in his own country and a prince. We took
the customs of his people and his experiences as the subject
of our lectures. I could sing, play the guitar, violin and
piano, but I did not know his native language. He began to
teach me and as soon as I could sing the song How Firm A
Foundation in his language which went this way:

```
          Ngama i-bata,Njami buyek
          Wema Wemeta, Negana i
          bukek diol, di Njami,
          i-diol de Kak
          Annimix, Annimix hanci

          Bata ba Satana i-bu butete
          Bata ba Npjami i bunanan
          Bata be satana ba laba i wa-
          Bata ba Njami ba laba Munonga
```

"We traveled and lectured in both the north and the
south and our life, while we had to work hard, was one of
happiness and contentment. I traveled and lectured as the
Princess Quango Hennadonah Perceriah, wife of the Abyssinian
Prince. I often recited the recitation written by the
colored poet, Paul Lawrence Dunbar <u>When</u> **Malinda** <u>Sings</u> to
the delight of our audiences.

The following incidents of African life were related
to me by my husband Quango Hennadonah Perceriah and they
were also given in his lectures on African customs while
touring the United States.

"The religion of the Bakuba tribe of Abyssinia was
almost wholly Pagan as the natives believed fully in witchcraft, sorcery, myths and superstitions. The witch doctor
held absolute sway over the members of the tribe and when
his reputation as a giver of rain, bountiful crops or
success in the chase was at stake the tribes were called
together and those accused by the witch doctor of being
responsible for these conditions through witchery were
condemed and speedily executed.

"The people were called together by the beating of
drums. The witch doctor, dressed in the most hellish garb
imaginable with his body painted and poisonous snake bone
necklaces dangling from his neck and the claws of
ferocious beasts, lions, leopards and the teeth of vicious
man-eating crocodiles finishing up his adornment, sat in

the middle of a court surrounded by the members of the
tribe. In his hand he carried a gourd which contained
beads, shot, or small stones. He began his incantations
by rattling the contents of the gourd, shouting and making
many weird wails and peculiar contortions. After this had
gone on for sometime until he was near exhaustion his face
assumed the expression of one in great pain and this was the
beginning of the end for some poor ignorant savage. He
squirmed and turned in different directions with his eyes
fixed with a set stare as if in expectancy when suddenly
his gaze would be fixed on some member of the tribe and his
finger pointed directly at him. The victim was at once
seized and bound, the doctor's gaze never leaving him until
this was done. If one victim appeased his nervous fervor
the trial was over but if his wrought-up feelings desired
more his screechings continued until a second victim was
secured. He had these men put to death to justify himself
in the eyes of the natives of his tribe for his failing to
bring rain, bountiful crops and success to the tribe.

"The witch doctor who sat as judge seemed to have
perfect control over the savages minds and no one questioned
his decisions. The persons were reconciled to their fate
and were led away to execution while they moaned and bade
their friends goodbye in the doleful savage style. Sometimes they were put on a boat, taken out into the middle
of a river and there cut to pieces with blades of grass,

their limbs being dismembered first and thrown into the
river to the crocodiles. A drink containing an opiate
was generally given the victim to deaden the pain but
often this formality was dispensed with. The victims were
often cut to pieces at the place of trial with knives and
their limbs thrown out to the vultures that almost con-
tinuously hover 'round the huts and kraals of the savage
tribes of Africa.

"In some instances condemned persons were burned at
the stake. This form of execution is meted out at some of
the religious dances or festivities to some of their pagan
gods to atone and drive away the evil spirits that have
caused pestilences to come upon the people. The victims
at these times are tortured in truly savage fashion, being
burned to death by degrees while the other members of the
tribe dance around and go wild with religious fervor calling
to their gods while the victim screeches with pain in his
slowly approaching death throes. Young girls, women, boys
and men are often accused of witchcraft. One method they
used of telling whether the victim accused was innocent or
guilty was to give them a liquid poison made from the juice
of several poisonous plants. If they could drink it and
live they were innocent, if they died they were guilty. In
most cases death was almost instantaneous. Some vomited
the poison from their stomachs and lived.

"The Bakubas sometimes resorted to cannibalism and

my husband told me of a Bakuba girl who ate her own mother.
Once a snake bit a man and he at once called the witch
doctor. The snake was a poisonous one and the man bitten
was in great pain. The witch doctor whooped and went through
several chants but the man got worse instead of better. The
witch doctor then told the man that his wife made the snake
bite him by witchery and that she should die for the act.
The natives gathered at once in response to the witch doctor's
call and the woman was executed at once. The man bitten by
the snake finally died but the witch doctor had shifted the
responsibility of his failure to help the man to his wife
who had been beheaded. The witch doctor had justified himself and the incident was closed.

"The tribe ruled by a King has two or more absolute
rules. The Kings word is law and he has the power to condemn
any subject to death at any time without trial. If he
becomes angry or offended with any of his wives a nod and a
word to his body guard and the woman is led away to execution.
Any person pf the tribe is subject to the King's will with
the exception of the witch doctor. Executions of a different nature than the ones described above are common occurances.
For general crimes the culprit after being condemned to death
is placed in a chair shaped very much like the electric chairs
used in American prisons in taking the lives of the condemned.
He is then tied firmly to the chair with thongs. A pole

made of a green sapling is firmly implanted in the earth
nearby. A thong is placed around the neck of the victim
under the chin. The sapling is then bent over and the
other end of the thong tied to the end of the sapling pole.
The pole stretches the neck to its full length and holds
the head erect. Drums are sometimes beaten to drown the
cries of those who are to be killed. The executioner who
is called a headsman then walks forward approaching the
chair from the rear. When he reaches it he steps to the
side of the victim and with a large, sharp, long-bladed knife
lopps off the head of the criminal. The bodies of men
executed in this manner are buried in shallow holes dug
about two feet deep to receive their bodies.

"The rank and file of the savage tribes believe ex-
plicitly in the supernatural powers of the witch doctor
and his decisions are not questioned. Not even the King
of the tribe raises a voice against him. The witch doctor
is crafty enough not to condemn any of the King's household
or any one directly prominent in the King's service. After
an execution everything is quiet in a few hours and the
incident seems forgotten. The African Negroes attitude
towards the whole affair seems to be instinctive and as long
as he escapes he does not show any particular concern in his
fellowman. His is of an animal instinctive nature.

"The males of the African tribes of savages have very
little respect for a woman but they demand a whole lot of

courtesies from their wives, beating them unmercifully
when they feel proper respect has not been shown them. The
men hunt game and make war on other tribes and the women
do all the work. A savage warrior when not engaged in
hunting or war, sleeps a lot and smokes almost continously
during his waking hours. Girls are bought from their parents
while mere children by the payment of so many cows, goats,etc.
The King can take any woman of the tribe whether married or
single he desires to be his wife. The parents of young girls
taken to wife by the King of a tribe feel honored and fall
on their knees and thank the King for taking her.

"The prince of a tribe is born a headsman and as soon
as he is able to wield a knife he is called upon to perform
the duty of cutting off the heads of criminals who are condemned to death by the King for general crimes. Those condemned by the witch doctor for witchcraft are executed by
dismemberment or fire as described above.

My husband was a cannibal headsman and performed this
duty of cutting off persons heads when a boy and after being
civilized in America this feature of his early life bore so
heavily upon his mind that it was instrumental in driving
him insane. By custom a prince was born a headsman and it
was compulsory that he execute criminals. He died in an
insane ward of the New Jersey State Hospital.

EH

N. C. District No. 2   Subject JANE ARRINGTON

Worker T. Pat Matthews   Story teller Jane Arrington

No. words   1051   Editor Geo. L. Andrews

JANE ARRINGTON
84 years old
302 Fowle Street
Raleigh, N. C.

"I ort to be able to tell sumpin cause I wus twelve
years old when dey had de surrender right up here in Raleigh.
If I live to see dis coming December I will be eighty five
years old. I wus born on the 18th of December 1852.

"I belonged to Jackson May of Nash County. I wus
born on de plantation near Tar River. Jackson May never
married until I wus of a great big girl. He owned a lot
of slaves; dere were eighty on de plantation before de
surrender. He married Miss Becky Wilder, sister of Sam
Wilder. De Wilders lived on a jining plantation to where
I wus borned.

"Jackson May had so many niggers he let Billy Williams
who had a plantation nearby have part of 'em. Marster
Jackson he raised my father and bought my mother. My
mother wus named Louisa May, and my father wus named Louis
May. My mother had six chilluns, four boys and two girls.
The boys were Richard, Farro, Caeser, and Fenner. De girls
Rose and Jane. Jane, dats me.

"We lived in log houses with stick an' dirt chimleys.
They called 'em the slave houses. We had chicken feather.

beds to sleep on an' de houses wus good warm comfortable
log houses. We had plenty of cover an' feather pillows.

"My grandmother on my mother's side told me a lot
of stories 'bout haints and how people run from 'em. Dey
told me 'bout slaves dat had been killed by dere marster's
coming back and worryin' 'em. Ole Missus Penny Williams,
before Jackson May bought mother, treated some of de slaves
mighty bad. She died an' den come back an' nearly scared
de slaves to death. Grandmother told all we chillun she
seed her an' knowed her after she been dead an' come back.

"John May a slave wus beat to death by Bill Stone
an' Oliver May. Oliver May wus Junius May's son. Junius
May wus Jackson May's Uncle. John May come back an' wurried
both of 'em. Dey could hardly sleep arter dat. Dey said
dey could hear him hollerin' an' groanin' most all de time.
Dese white men would groan in dere sleep an' tell John to
go away. Dey would say, 'Go way John, please go away'. De
other slaves wus afraid of 'em cause de ghost of John wurried
'em so bad.

"I wurked on de farm, cuttin' corn stalks and tendin'
to cattle in slavery time. Sometimes I swept de yards. I
never got any money for my work and we didn't have any patches.
My brothers caught possums, coons and sich things an' we

cooked 'em in our houses. We had no parties but we had quiltin's. We went to the white folks church, Peach Tree Church, six miles from de plantation an' Poplar Springs Church seven miles away. Both were missionary Baptist Churches.

"There were no overseers on Jackson May's plantation. He wouldn't have nary one. Billy Williams didn't have none. Dey had colored slave foremen.

"After wurkin' all day dere wus a task of cotton to be picked an' spun by 'em. Dis wus two onces of cotton. Some of de slaves run away from Bill Williams when Marster Jackson May let him have 'em to work. Dey run away an', come home. Aunt Chaney runned away an' mother run away. Marster Jackson May kept 'em hid cause he say dey wus not treated right. He wouldn't let 'em **have** 'em back no more.

"I never saw a grown slave whupped or in chains and I never saw a slave sold. Jackson May would not sell a slave. He didn't think it right. He kept 'em together. He had **eighty head**. He would let other white people have 'em to wurk for 'em sometimes, but he would not sell none of 'em.

"If dey caught a slave wid a book you knowed it meant a whuppin', but de white chillun teached slaves secretey sometimes. Ole man Jake Rice a slave who belonged to John Rice in Nash County wus teached by ole John Rice's son till he had a purty good mount of larnin'.

"We did not have prayer meeting at marster's plantation or anywhur. Marster would not allow dat.

"When I wus a child we played de games of three handed reels, 'Old Gray Goose', 'All Little Gal, All Little Gal, All Little Gal remember me'. We took hold of hands an' run round as we sang dis song.

"We sang 'Old Dan Tucker'. Git outen de way, ole Dan Tucker, Sixteen Hosses in one stable, one jumped out an' skined his nable an' so on.

"Dr. Mann and Dr. Sid Harris and Dr. Fee Mann and Dr. Mathias looked arter us when we wus sick. Mother and de other grown folks raised herbs dat dey give us too. Chillun took a lot of salts.

"Jackson May wus too rich to go to de war. Billy Williams didn't go, too rich too, I reckons. I remember when dey said niggers had to be free. De papers said if dey could not be freedom by good men dere would be freedom by blood. Dey fighted an' kept on fightin' a long time.

Den de Yankees come. I heard dem beat de drum. Marster tole us we wus free but mother an' father stayed on with Marster. He promised 'em sumptin, but he give 'em nothin'. When de crop wus housed dey left.

"Father and mother went to Hench Stallings plantation and stayed there one year. Then they went to Jim Webbs farm. I don't remember how long they stayed there but round two years. They moved about an' about among the white folks till they died. They never owned any property. They been dead 'bout thirty years.

"I married Sidney Arrington. He has been dead six years las' September.

"I am unable to do any kind of work. My arm is mighty weak.

"I know slavery wus a bad thing. I don't have to think anything about it. Abraham Lincoln wus the first of us bein' free. I think he wus a man of God. I think Roosevelt is all right man. I belongs to the Penticostial Holliness Church."

AC

N. C. District No. 2   Subject <u>SARAH LOUISE AUGUSTUS</u>

Worker <u>T. Pat Matthews</u>   Source <u>Sarah Louise Augustus</u>

No. Words <u>1,426</u>   Editor <u>George L. Andrews</u>

SARAH LOUISE AUGUSTUS
Age 80 years
1424 Lane Street
Raleigh, North Carolina

"I wus born on a plantation near Fayetteville, N. C.,
and I belonged to J. B. Smith. His wife wus named Henrietta.
He owned about thirty slaves. When a slave wus no good he
wus put on the auction block in Fayetteville and sold.

"My father wus named Romeo Harden and my mother wus
named Alice Smith. The little cabin where I wus born is
still standing.

"There wus seven children in marster's family, four
girls and two boys. The girls wus named Ellen, Ida, Mary
and Elizabeth. The boys wus named Harry, Norman and Marse
George. Marse George went to the war. Mother had a family
of four girls. Their names wus: Mary, Kate, Hannah and
myself, Sarah Louise. I am the only one living and I would
not be living but I have spent most of my life in white folk's
houses and they have looked after me. I respected myself
and they respected me.

"My first days of slavery wus hard. I slept on a
pallet on the floor of the cabin and just as soon as I wus

able to work any at all I wus put to milking cows.

"I have seen the paterollers hunting men and have
seen men they had whipped. The slave block stood in the
center of the street, Fayetteville Street, where Ramsey and
Gillespie Street came in near Cool Springs Street. The silk
mill stood just below the slave market. I saw the silkworms
that made the silk and saw them gather the cocoons and spin
the silk.

"They hung people in the middle of Ramsey Street.
They put up a gallows and hung the men exactly at 12 o'clock.

"I ran away from the plantation once to go with some
white children to see a man hung.

"The only boats I remember on the Cape Fear wus the
Governor Worth, The Hurt, The Iser and The North State.
Oh! Lord yes, I remember the stage coach. As many times
as I run to carry the mail to them when they come by!
They blew a horn before they got there and you had to be
on time 'cause they could not wait. There wus a stage each
way each day, one up and one down.

"Mr. George Lander had the first Tombstone Marble
yard in Fayetteville on Hay Street on the point of Flat
Iron place. Lander wus from Scotland. They gave me a pot,

a scarf, and his sister gave me some shells. I have all
the things they gave me. My missus, Henrietta Smith, wus
Mr. Lander's sister. I waited on the Landers part of the
time. They were hard working white folks, honest, God
fearing people. The things they gave me were brought from
over the sea.

"I can remember when there wus no hospital in
Fayetteville. There wus a little place near the depot
where there wus a board shanty where they operated on
people. I stood outside once and saw the doctors take a
man's leg off. Dr. McDuffy wus the man who took the leg
off. He lived on Hay Street near the Silk Mill.

"When one of the white folks died they sent slaves
around to the homes of their friends and neighbors with
a large sheet of paper with a piece of black crepe pinned
to the top of it. The friends would sign or make a cross
mark on it. The funerals were held at the homes and friends
and neighbors stood on the porch and in the house while the
services were going on. The bodies were carried to the
grave after the services in a black hearse drawn by black
horses. If they did not have black horses to draw the
hearse they went off and borrowed them. The colored people

washed and shrouded the dead bodies. My grandmother wus
one who did this. Her name wus Sarah McDonald. She
belonged to Capt. George McDonald. She had fifteen children
and lived to be one hundred and ten years old. She died
in Fayetteville of pneumonia. She wus in Raleigh nursing
the Briggs family, Mrs. F. H. Briggs' family. She wus
going home to Fayetteville when she wus caught in a rain
storm at Sanford, while changing trains. The train for
Fayetteville had left as the train for Sanford wus late
so she stayed wet all night. Next day she went home,
took pneumonia and died. She wus great on curing rheumatism;
she did it with herbs. She grew hops and other herbs and
cured many people of this disease.

"She wus called black mammy because she wet nursed
so many white children. In slavery time she nursed all
babies hatched on her marster's plantation and kept it up
after the war as long as she had children.

"Grandfather wus named Isaac Fuller. Mrs. Mary
Ann Fuller, Kate Fuller, Mr. Will Fuller, who wus a lawyer
in Wall Street, New York, is some of their white folks.
The Fullers were born in Fayetteville. One of the slaves,
Dick McAlister, worked, saved a small fortune and left it

to Mr. Will Fuller. People thought the slave ought to
have left it to his sister but he left it to Mr. Will.
Mr. Fuller gives part of it to the ex-slaves sister each
year. Mr. Will always helped the Negroes out when he
could. He wus good to Dick and Dick McAlister gave him
all his belongings when he died.

"The Yankees came through Fayetteville wearing
large blue coats with capes on them. Lots of them were
mounted, and there were thousands of foot soldiers. It
took them several days to get through town. The Southern
soldiers retreated and then in a few hours the Yankees
covered the town. They busted into the smokehouse at
marster's, took the meat, meal and other provisions.
Grandmother pled with the Yankees but it did no good.
They took all they wanted. They said if they had to
come again they would take the babies from the cradles.
They told us we were all free. The Negroes begun visiting
each other in the cabins and became so excited they began
to shout and pray. I thought they were all crazy.

"We stayed right on with marster. He had a town
house and a big house on the plantation. I went to the
town house to work, but mother and grandmother stayed on

the plantation. My mother died there and the white folks
buried her. Father stayed right on and helped run the
farm until he died. My uncle, Elic Smith, and his family
stayed too. Grandfather and grandmother after a few years
left the plantation and went to live on a little place
which Mrs. Mary Ann Fuller gave them. Grandmother and
grandfather died there.

"I wus thirty years old when I married. I wus
married in my missus' graduating dress. I wus married
in the white folks' church, to James Henry Harris. The
white folks carried me there and gave me away. Miss Mary
Smith gave me away. The wedding wus attended mostly by
white folks.

"My husband wus a fireman on the Cape Fear River
boats and a white man's Negro too. We had two children,
both died while little. My husband and I spent much of
our time with the white folks and when he wus on his runs
I slept in their homes. Often the children of the white
families slept with me. We both tried to live up to the
standards of decency and honesty and to be worthy of the
confidence placed in us by our white folks.

"My husband wus finally offered a job with a shipping
concern in Deleware and we moved there. He wus fireman on

the freighter Wilmington. He worked there three years,
when he wus drowned. After his death I married David
Augustus and immediately came back to North Carolina and
my white folks, and we have been here ever since. I am
a member of several Negro Lodges and am on the Committee
for the North Carolina Colored State Fair.

"There are only a few of the old white folks who
have always been good to me living now, but I am still
working with their offspring, among whom I have some
mighty dear friends. I wus about eight years old when
Sherman's Army came through. Guess I am about eighty
years of age now."

N. C. District   # 2   Subject: A Slave Story

No. Words: 908   Story Teller: Charity Austin

Worker: Ma Pat Matthews   Editor: Daisy Bailey Waitt

CHARITY AUSTIN

507 South Bloodworth Street, Raleigh, N.C.

" I wus borned in the year 1852, July 27. I wus
born in Granville County, sold to a slave speculator at
ten years old and carried to Southwest, Georgia. I belonged
to Samuel Howard. His daughter took me to Kinston, North
Carolina and I stayed there until I wus sold. She married a
man named Bill Brown, and her name wus Julia Howard Brown.
My father wus named Paul Howard and my mother wus named
Chollie Howard. My old missus wus named Polly Howard.

"John Richard Keine from Danville, Virginia bought me
and sent me to a plantation in Georgia. We only had a white
overseer there, He and his wife and children lived on the
plantation. We had slave quarters there. Slaves were
bought up and sent there in chains. Some were chained to
each other by the legs, some by the arms. They called the
leg chains shackles. I have lived a hard life. I have
seen mothers sold away from their babies and other children,
and they cryin' when she left. I have seen husbands sold
from their wives, and wives sold from their husbands.

"Abraham Lincoln came through once, but none of us
knew who he wus. He wus just the raggedest man you ever saw.

The white children and me saw him out at the railroad. We
were settin' and waitin' to see him. He said he wus huntin'
his people; and dat he had lost all he had. Dey give him
somethin' to eat and tobacco to chew, and he went on. Soon
we heard he wus in de White House then we knew who it wus
come through. We knowed den it wus Abraham Lincoln.

"We children stole eggs and sold 'em durin' slavery.
Some of de white men bought 'em. They were Irishmen and
they would not tell on us. Their names were Mulligan, Flanagan
and Dugan. They wore good clothes and were funny mens.
They called guns flutes.

"Boss tole us Abraham Lincoln wus dead and we were
still slaves. Our boss man bought black cloth and made us
wear it for mourning for Abraham Lincoln and tole us that
there would not be freedom. We stayed there another year
after freedom. A lot o' de niggers knowed nothin' 'cept what
missus and marster tole us. What dey said wus just de same
as de Lawd had spoken to us.

"Just after de surrender a nigger woman who wus bad,
wus choppin' cotton at out plantation in Georgie. John
Woodfox wus de main overseer and his son-in-law wus a overseer. Dey had a colored man who dey called a nigger driver.
De nigger driver tole de overseer de woman wus bad. De overseer came to her, snatched de hoe from her and hit her. The

blow killed her. He wus reported to de Freedman's Bureau.
Dey came, whupped de overseer and put him in jail. Dey
decided not to kill him, but made him furnish de children
of de dead woman so much to live on. Dere wus a hundred or
more niggers in de field when this murder happened.

"We finally found out we were free and left. Dey
let me stay with Miss Julia Brown. I wus hired to her.
She lived in Dooley County, Georgie. I next worked with
Mrs. Dunbar after after staying with Mrs. Brown four years.
Her name wus Mrs. Minnie Dunbar and she moved to Columbia,
South Carolina takin' me with her. I stayed with her about
four years. This wus the end of my maiden life. I married
Isaac Austin of Richmond County, Georgie. He wus a native of
Warrenton County and he brought me from his home in Richmond
County, Georgie to Warrenton and then from Warrenton to
Raleigh. I had two brothers and thirteen sisters. I did
general house work, and helped raise children during slavery,
and right after de war. Then you had to depend on yourself
to do for children. You had to doctor and care for them yourself. You just had to depend on yourself.

"Dey had 320 acres o' cleared fields in Georgie and
then de rice fields, I just don't know how many acres. I
have seen jails for slaves. Dey had a basement for a jail
in Georgie and a guard at de holes in it.

"No, No! you better not be caught tryin' to do somethin'
wid a book. Dey would teach you wid a stick or switch. De
slaves had secret prayer meetin's wid pots turned down to
kill de soun' o' de singin'. We sang a song, 'I am glad
salvation's free.' Once dey heard us, nex' mornin' dey
took us and tore our backs to pieces. Dey would say, 'Are
you free? What were you singin' about freedom?' While
de niggers were bein' whupped they said, 'Pray, marster, pray.'

"The doctor came to see us sometimes when we were
sick, but not after. People just had to do their own doctor-
in' . Sometimes a man would take his patient, and sit by de road
where de doctor travelled, and when he come along he would
see him. De doctor rode in a sully drawn by a horse. He had
a route, one doctor to two territories.

"When de white folks were preparing to go to de war
they had big dinners and speakin'. Dey tole what dey were
goin' to do to Sherman and Grant. A lot of such men as Grant
and Sherman and Lincoln came through de South in rags and were
at some o' dese meetings, an' et de dinners. When de white
folks foun' it out , dere wus some sick folks. Sometimes we
got two days Christmas and two days July. When de nigger wus
freed dey didn't know where to go and what to do. It wus hard,
but it has been hard since. From what de white folks, marster and
missus tole us we thought Lincoln wus terrible. By what mother
and father tole me I thought he wus all right. I think
Roosevelt wus put in by God to do the right thing."

N. C. District __No. 2__   Subject _____BLOUNT BAKER_____

Worker __Mary A. Hicks__   Person Interviewed __Blount Baker__

No. Words __367__   Editor _____G. L. Andrews_____

BLOUNT BAKER

An interview with Blount Baker, 106 Spruce Street, Wilson,
North Carolina.

"Yes'um, I 'longed ter Marse Henry Allen of Wilson
County an' we always raise terbacker. Marse Henry wus good
ter us so we had a heap of prayer meetin's an' corn shuckin's
an' such.

"I 'members de big meetin's dat we'd have in de summer time
an' dat good singin' we'd have when we'd be singin' de sinners
through. We'd stay pretty nigh all night to make a sinner come
through, an' maybe de week atter de meetin' he'd steal one of
his marster's hogs. Yes'um, I'se had a bad time.

"You know, missy, dar ain't no use puttin' faith in nobody,
dey'd fool you ever time anyhow. I know once a patteroller
tol' me dat iffen I'd give him a belt I found dat he'd let me
go by ter see my gal dat night, but when he kotch me dat night
he whupped me. I tol' Marse Henry on him too so Marse Henry
takes de belt away from him an' gives me a possum fer hit.
Dat possum shore wus good too, baked in de ashes like I done it.

"I ain't never hear Marse Henry cuss but once an' dat wus
de time dat some gentlemens come ter de house an' sez dat dar
am a war 'twixt de north an' de south. He sez den, 'Let de
damn yaller bellied Yankees come on an' we'll give 'em hell
an' sen' dem a-hoppin' back ter de north in a hurry.'

"We ain't seed no Yankees 'cept a few huntin' Rebs. Dey talk mean ter us an' one of dem says dat we niggers am de cause of de war. 'Sir,' I sez, 'folks what am a wantin' a war can always find a cause'. He kicks me in de seat of de pants fer dat, so I hushes.

"I stayed wid Marse Henry till he died den I moved ter Wilson. I has worked everwhere, terbacker warehouses an' ever'thing. I'se gittin' of my ole age pension right away an' den de county won't have ter support me no mo', dat is if dey have been supportin' me on three dollars a month."

LE

N. C. District__No. 2__   Subject_____LIZZIE BAKER_____

Worker__T. Pat Matthews   Person Interviewed_Lizzie Baker__

No. Words___745_____   Editor_Daisy Bailey Waitt_____

LIZZIE BAKER
424 Smith Street

"I was born de las' year o' de surrender an'course I
don't remember seein' any Yankee soldiers, but I knows
a plenty my mother and father tole me. I have neuritus,
an' have been unable to work any fer a year and fer seven
years I couldn't do much.

"My mother wus named Teeny McIntire and my father
William McIntire. Mammy belonged to Bryant Newkirk in
Duplin County. Pap belonged to someone else, I don't
know who.

"Dey said dey worked from light till dark, and pap
said dey beat him so bad he run away a lot o' times. Dey
said de paterollers come to whare dey wus havin' prayer
meetin' and beat 'em.

"Mammy said sometimes dey were fed well and others
dey almost starved. Dey got biscuit once a week on Sunday. Dey said dey went to de white folks's church. Dey
said de preachers tole 'em dey had to obey dere missus
and marster. My mammy said she didn't go to no dances
'cause she wus crippled. Some o' de help, a colored woman,
stole something when she wus hongry. She put it off on
mother and missus made mother wear trousers for a year to

punish her.

"Mammy said dey gave de slaves on de plantation
one day Christmas and dat New Years wus when dey
sold 'em an' hired 'em out. All de slaves wus scared
'cause dey didn't know who would have to go off to be
sold or to work in a strange place. Pap tole me 'bout
livin' in de woods and 'bout dey ketchin' him. I member
his owner's name den, it wus Stanley. He run away so
bad dey sold him several times. Pap said one time dey
caught him and nearly beat him to death, and jest as
soon as he got well and got a good chance he ran away
again.

"Mammy said when de Yankees come through she wus
'fraid of 'em. De Yankees tole her not to be 'fraid of
'em. Dey say to her, 'Do dey treat you right', Mammy
said 'Yes sir', 'cause ole missus wus standin' dere, an'
she wus 'fraid not to say yes. Atter de war, de fust
year atter de surrender dey moved to James Alderman's
place in Duplin County and stayed dere till I wus a
grown gal.

"Den we moved to Goldsboro. Father wus a carpenter
and he got a lot of dat work. Dat's what he done in
Goldsboro. We come from Goldsboro to Raleigh and we have
lived here every since. We moved here about de year o'
de shake and my mother died right here in Raleigh de year
o' de shake. Some of de things mother tole me 'bout
slavery has gone right out of my min'. Jes comes and
goes.

"I remember pap tellin' me 'bout stretchin' vines
acrost roads and paths to knock de patterollers off deir
horses when dey were tryin' to ketch slaves. Pap and
mammy tole me marster and missus did not 'low any of de
slaves to have a book in deir house. Dat if dey caught a
slave wid a book in deir house dey whupped 'em. Dey
were keerful not to let 'em learn readin' and writin'.

"Dey sold my sister Lucy and my brother Fred in
slavery time, an' I have never seen 'em in my life.
Lother would cry when she was tellin' me 'bout it. She
never seen 'em anymore. I jes' couldn't bear to hear
her tell it widout cryin'. Dey were carried to Richmond, an' sold by old marster when dey were chillun.

"We tried to get some news of brother and sister.
Lother kept 'quiring 'bout 'em as long as she lived and
I have hoped dat I could hear from 'em. Dey are dead
long ago I recons, and I guess dare aint no use ever
expectin' to see 'em. Slavery wus bad and Mr. Lincoln
did a good thing when he freed de niggers. I caint ex-
press my love for Roosevelt. He has saved so many lives.
I think he has saved mine. I want to see him face to
face. I purely love him and I feel I could do better to
see him and tell him so face to face.

LE

N. C. District <u>No. 2</u>　　　　Subject <u>VINEY BAKER</u>

Worker <u>Mary A. Hicks</u>　　　Story teller <u>Viney Baker</u>

No. Words <u>339</u>　　　　　　Editor <u>Daisy Bailey Waitt</u>

VINEY BAKER
Ex-Slave Story

An interview with Viney Baker 78 of S. Harrington Street,
Raleigh.
R

"My mammy wuz Hannah Murry an' so fur as I know I
ain't got no father, do' I reckon dat he wuz de plantation
stock nigger. I wuz borned in Virginia as yo' mought say
ter my marster Mr. S. L. Allen.

"We moved when I wuz little ter Durham County whar
we fared bad. We ain't had nothin' much ter eat an' ter
w'ar. He had a hundert slaves an' I reckon five hundert
acres o' lan'. He made us wuck hard, de little ones
included.

"One night I lay down on de straw mattress wid
my mammy, an' de nex' mo'nin' I woked up an' she wuz gone.
When I axed 'bout her I fin's dat a speculator comed dar
de night before an' wanted ter buy a 'oman. Dey had come
an' got my mammy widout wakin' me up. I has always been
glad somehow dat I wuz asleep.

"Dey uster tie me ter a tree an' beat me till de
blood run down my back, I doan 'member nothin' dat I done,

I jist 'members de whuppin's. Some of de rest wuz beat
wuser dan I wuz too, an' I uster scream dat I wuz sho'
dyin'.

  "Yess'um I seed de Yankees go by, but dey ain't
bodder us none, case dey knows dat 'hind eber' bush jist
about a Confederate soldier pints a gun.

  "I warn't glad at de surrender, case I doan
understand hit, an' de Allen's keeps me right on, an'
whups me wuser den dan eber.

  "I reckon I wuz twelve years old when my mammy
come ter de house an' axes Mis' Allen ter let me go spen'
de week en' wid her. Mis' Allen can't say no, case Mammy
mought go ter de carpet baggers so she lets me go fer de
week-en'. Mammy laughs Sunday when I says somethin' 'bout
goin' back. Naw, I stayed on wid my mammy, an' I ain't
seed Mis' Allen no mo'."

AC

District   # 2   Subject: EX-SLAVE STORY

No Words: 733   Story teller: Charlie Barbour

Worker: Mary A. Hicks   Editor: Daisy Bailey Waitt

EX-SLAVE STORY

An interview on May 20,1937 with Charlie Barbour, 86 of
Smithfield, N.C. Johnston County.

"I belonged ter Mr. Bob Lumsford hyar in Smithfield
from de time of my birth. My mammy wuz named Candice an'
my pappy's name wuz Seth. My brothers wuz Rufus, William
an' George, an' my sisters wuz Mary an' Laura.

"I 'minds me of de days when as a young]n' I played
marbles an' hide an' seek. Dar wuzn't many games den, case
nobody ain't had no time fer 'em. De grown folkses had
dances an' sometimes co'n shuckin's, an' de little niggers
patted dere feets at de dances an' dey he'p ter shuck de
co'n. At Christmas we had a big dinner, an' from den through
New Year's Day we feast, an' we dance, an' we sing. De fust
one what said Christmas gift ter anybody else got a gif', so
of cou'se we all try ter ketch de marster.

"On de night 'fore de first day of Jinuary we had a
dance what lasts all night. At nidnight when de New Year
comes in marster makes a speech an' we is happy dat he
thanks us fer our year's wuck an' says dat we is good, smart
slaves.

"Marster wucked his niggers from daylight till dark, an'

his thirteen grown slaves had ter ten' 'bout three hundred acres o' land. Course dey mostly planted co'n, peas an' vege'ables.

"I can 'member, do' I wuz small, dat de slaves wuz whupped fer disobeyin' an' I can think of seberal dat I got. I wuz doin' housewuck at de time an' one of de silber knives got misplaced. Dey ' cused me of misplacin' it on purpose, so I got de wust beatin' dat I eber had. I wuz beat den till de hide wuz busted hyar an' dar.

"We little ones had some time ter go swimmin' an' we did; we also fished, an' at night we hunted de possum an' de coon sometimes. Ole Uncle Jeems had some houn's what would run possums or coons an' he uster take we boys 'long wid him.

"I 'members onct de houn's struck a trail an' dey tree de coon. Uncle Jeems sen's Joe, who wuz bigger den I wuz, up de tree ter ketch de coon an' he warns him dat coons am fightin' fellers. Joe doan pay much mind he am so happy ter git der chanct ter ketch de coon, but when he ketched dat coon he couldn't turn loose, an' from de way he holler yo' would s'pose dat he ain't neber wanted ter ketch a coon. When Joe Barbour wuz buried hyar las' winter dem coon marks wuz still strong on his arms an' han's an' dar wuz de long scar on his face.

"I 'members onct a Yankee 'oman from New York looks at him an' nigh 'bout faints. 'I reckon', says she,'dat dat am what de cruel slave owner or driver done ter him'.

"Yes mam, I knows when de Yankees comed ter Smithfield.
Dey comed wid de beatin' of drums an' de wavin' of flags.
Dey says dat our governor wuz hyar makin' a speech but he
flewed 'fore dey got hyar. Anyhow, we libed off from de
main path of march, an' so we ain't been trouble so much
'cept by 'scootin' parties, as my ole missus call 'em.

" Dey am de darndest yo' eber seed, dey won't eat no
hog meat 'cept hams an' shoulders an' dey goes ter de smoke
house an' gits 'em 'thout no permission. Dey has what dey
calls rammin' rods ter dere guns an' dey knock de chickens
in de haid wid dat. I hyard dem say dat dar warn't no use
wastin' powder on dem chickens.

"Dey went ober de neighborhood stealin' an' killin'
stock. I hyard 'bout 'em ketchin' a pig, cuttin' off his
hams an' leave him dar alive. De foun' all de things we
done hid, not dat I thinks dat dey am witches, but dat dey
has a money rod, an' 'cides dat some of de slaves tol' 'em
whar marster had hid de things.

"Yes 'um, I reckon I wuz glad ter git free, case I
knows den dat I won't wake up some mornin' ter fin' dat my
mammy or some ob de rest of my family am done sold. I left
de day I hyard 'bout de surrender an' I fared right good
too, do' I knows dem what ain't farin' so well.

"I ain't neber learn ter read an' write an' I knows
now dat I neber will. I can't eben write a letter ter
Raleigh 'bout my ole man's pension.

"I 'members de days when mammy wored a blue hankerchief
'round her haid an' cooked in de great house. She'd sometimes sneak me a cookie or a cobbler an' fruits. She had
her own little gyardin an' a few chickens an' we w'oud ov
been happy 'cept dat we wuz skeered o' bein' sold.

"I'se glad dat slavery am ober, case now de nigger has
got a chanct ter live an' larn wid de whites. Dey won't neber
be as good as de whites but dey can larn ter live an' enjoy
life more.

"Speakin' 'bout de Ku Klux dey ain't do nothin' but
scare me back in '69, but iffen we had some now I thinks dat
some of dese young niggers what has forgot what dey mammies
tol' 'em would do better."

MH/EH

N. C. District No. 2   Subject   MARY BARBOUR

Worker Mary A. Hicks   Person Interviewed Mary Barbour

No. Words   678   Editor Daisy Bailey Waitt

MARY BARBOUR

Ex-Slave Story

An interview with Mary Barbour 81 of 801 S. Bloodworth
Street, Raleigh, N. C.

"I reckon dat I wuz borned in McDowell County, case
dat's whar my mammy, Edith, lived. She 'longed ter Mr.
Jefferson Mitchel dar, an' my pappy 'longed ter er Mr.
Jordan in Avery County, so he said.

"'Fore de war, I doan know nothin' much 'cept dat we
lived on a big plantation an' dat my mammy wucked hard,
but wuz treated pretty good.

"We had our little log cabin off ter one side, an'
my mammy had sixteen chilluns. Fas' as dey got three years
old de marster sol' 'em till we las' four dat she had wid
her durin' de war. I wuz de oldes' o' dese four; den dar
wuz Henry an' den de twins, Liza an' Charlie.

"One of de fust things dat I 'members wuz my pappy
wakin' me up in de middle o' de night, dressin' me in de
dark, all de time tellin' me ter keep quiet. One o' de
twins hollered some an' pappy put his hand ober its mouth
ter keep it quiet.

"Atter we wuz dressed he went outside an' peeped roun' fer a minute den he comed back an' got us. We snook out o' de house an' long de woods path, pappy totin' one of de twins an' holdin' me by de han' an' mammy carryin' de udder two.

"I reckons dat I will always 'member dat walk, wid de bushes slappin' my laigs, de win' sighin' in de trees, an' de hoot owls an' whippoorwhills hollerin' at each other frum de big trees. I wuz half asleep an' skeered stiff, but in a little while we pass de plum' thicket an' dar am de mules an' wagin.

"Dar am er quilt in de bottom o' de wagin, an' on dis dey lays we youngins. An' pappy an' mammy gits on de board cross de front an' drives off down de road.

"I wuz sleepy but I wuz skeered too, so as we rides 'long I lis'ens ter pappy an' mammy talk. Pappy wuz tellin' mammy 'bout de Yankees comin' ter dere plantation, burnin' de co'n cribs, de smokehouses an' 'stroyin' eber'thing. He says right low dat dey done took marster Jordan ter de Rip Raps down nigh Norfolk, an' dat he stol' de mules an' wagin an' 'scaped.

"We wuz skeerd of de Yankees ter start wid, but de more we thinks 'bout us runnin' way frum our marsters de skeerder

we gits o' de Rebs. Anyhow pappy says dat we is goin ' ter
jine de Yankees.

"We trabels all night an' hid in de woods all day fer
a long time, but atter awhile we gits ter Doctor Billard's
place, in Chowan County. I reckons dat we stays dar seberal
days.

"De Yankees has tooked dis place so we stops ober, an'
has a heap o' fun dancin' a n' sich while we am dar. De
Yankees tells pappy ter head fer New Bern an' dat he will
be took keer of dar, so ter New Bern we goes.

"When we gits ter New Bern de Yankees takes de mules
an' wagin, dey tells pappy something, an' he puts us on a
long white boat named Ocean Waves an' ter Roanoke we goes.

"Later I larns dat most o' de reffes[1] is put in James
City, nigh New Bern, but dar am a pretty good crowd on
Roanoke. Dar wuz also a ole Indian Witch 'oman dat I 'mem-
bers.

"Atter a few days dar de Ocean Waves comes back an'
takes all ober ter New Bern. My pappy wuz a shoemaker, so
he makes Yankee boots, an' we gits 'long pretty good.

"I wuz raised in New Bern an' I lived dar till forty
years ago when me an' my husban' moved ter Raleigh an' do'
he's been daid a long time I has lived hyar ober since an'
eben if'en I is eighty-one years old I can still outwuck
my daughter an' de rest of dese young niggers."

1. refugees

N. C. District <u>No. 2</u>　　　　Subject <u>Plantation Times</u>

Worker <u>Mary A. Hicks</u>　　　Person Interviewed <u>Alice Baugh</u>

No. Words <u>927</u>　　　　　　Editor <u>Daisy Bailey Waitt</u>

PLANTATION TIMES

An Interview on May 18, 1937 with **Alice Baugh**, 84, who remembers hearing her mother tell of slavery days.

"My mammy Ferbie, an' her brother Darson belonged ter
Mr. David Hinnant in Edgecombe County till young Marster
Charlie got married. Den dey wuz drawed an' sent wid him
down hyar ter Wendell. De ole Hinnant home am still
standin' dar ter dis day.

"Marster Charlie an' Missus Mary wuz good ter de
hundred slaves what belonged ter 'em. Dey gib 'em good
houses, good feed, good clothes an' plenty uv fun. Dey
had dere co'n shuckin's, dere barn dances, prayer meetin's
an' sich like all de year, an' from Christmas till de
second day o' January dey had a holiday wid roast oxes,
pigs, turkey an' all de rest o' de fixin's. From Saturday
till Monday de slaves wuz off an' dey had dere Sunday
clothes, which wuz nice. De marster always gib 'em a
paper so's de patterollers won't git 'em.

"Dey went up de riber to other plantations ter dances
an' all dem things, an' dey wuz awful fond uv singin' songs.
Dat's whut dey done atter dey comes ter dere cabins at de
end o' de day. De grown folkses sings an' somebody pick
de banjo. De favorite song wuz 'Swing Low Sweet Chariot'
an' 'Play on yo' Harp Little David'. De chilluns uster

play Hide an' Seek, an' Leap Frog, an' ever'body wuz happy.

"Dey had time off ter hunt an' fish an' dey had dere own chickens, pigs, watermillons an' gyardens. De fruits from de big orchard an' de honey from de hives wuz et at home, an' de slave et as good as his marster et. (Dey had a whole heap of bee hives an' my mammy said dat she had ter tell dem bees when Mis' Mary died. She said how she wuz cryin' so hard dat she can't hardly tell 'em, an' dat dey hum lak dey am mo'nin' too.)

"My mammy marry my pappy dar an' she sez dat de preacher from de Methodis' Church marry 'em, dat she w'ar Miss Mary's weddin' dress, all uv white lace, an' dat my pappy w'ar Mr. Charlie's weddin' suit wid a flower in de button hole. Dey gived a big dance atter de supper dey had, an' Marster Charlie dance de fust set wid my mammy.

"I jist thought of a tale what I hyard my mammy tell 'bout de Issue Frees of Edgecombe County when she wuz a little gal. She said dat de Issue Frees wuz mixed wid de white folks, an' uv cou'se dat make 'em free. Sometimes dey stay on de plantation, but a whole heap uv dem, long wid niggers who had done runned away from dere marster, dugged caves in de woods, an' dar dey lived an' raised dere famblies dar. Dey ain 't wored much clothes an' what dey got to eat an' to w'ar dey swiped from de white folkses. Mammy said dat she uster go ter de spring fer

water, an' dem ole Issue Frees up in de woods would yell
at her, 'Doan yo' muddy dat spring, little gal'. Dat
scared her moughty bad.

"Dem Issue Frees till dis day shows both bloods. De
white folkses won't have 'em an' de niggers doan want 'em
but will have ter have 'em anyhow.

"My uncle wuz raised in a cave an' lived on stold
stuff an' berries. My cousin runned away 'cause his
marster wuz mean ter him, but dey put de blood hounds on
his trail, ketched him. Atter he got well from de beatin'
dey gib him, dey sold him.

"I'se hyard ole lady Prissie Jones who died at de
age of 103 las' winter tell 'bout marsters dat when dere
slaves runned away dey'd set de bloodhounds on dere trail
an' when dey ketched 'em dey'd cut dere haids off wid de
swords.

"Ole lady Prissie tole 'bout slaves what ain't had
nothin' ter eat an' no clothes 'cept a little strip uv
homespun, but my mammy who died four months ago at de age
106 said dat she ain't knowed nothin' 'bout such doin's.

"When de Yankees come, dey come a burnin' an' a-
stealin' an' Marster Charlie carried his val'ables ter
mammy's cabin, but dey found 'em. Dey had a money rod an'
dey'd find all de stuff no matter whar it wuz.

Mammy said dat all de slaves cried when de Yankees come,
an' dat most uv 'em stayed on a long time atter de war.
My mammy plowed an' done such work all de time uv slavery,
but she done it case she wanted to do it an' not 'cause
dey make her.

"All de slaves hate de Yankees an' when de southern
soldiers comed by late in de night all de niggers got
out of de bed an' holdin' torches high dey march behin'
de soldiers, all of dem singin', 'We'll Hang Abe Lincoln
on de Sour Apple Tree.' Yes mam, dey wuz sorry dat dey
wuz free, an' dey ain't got no reason tu be glad, case dey
wuz happier den dan now.

"I'se hyard mammy tell 'bout how de niggers would
sing as dey picked de cotton, but yo' ain't hyard none
uv dat now. Den dey ain't had to worry 'bout nothin;
now dey has ter study so much dat dey ain't happy nuff
ter sing no mo'!"

"Does yo' know de cause of de war?" Aunt Alice went
to a cupboard and returned holding out a book. "Well
hyar's de cause, dis Uncle Tom's Cabin wuz de cause
of it all, an' its' de biggest lie what ever been gived
ter de public."

N. C. District <u>No. 2</u>   Subject <u>WHEN THE YANKEES CAME</u>

Worker <u>Mary A. Hicks</u>   Story teller <u>John Beckwith</u>

No. Words <u>341</u>   Editor <u>Daisy Bailey Waitt</u>

WHEN THE YANKEES CAME

An Interview with John Beckwith 83, of Cary.

"I reckon dat I wuz 'bout nine years old at de
surrender, but we warn't happy an' we stayed on dar till
my parents died. My pappy wuz named Green an' my mammy
wuz named Molly, an' we belonged ter Mr. Joe Edwards, Mr.
Marion Gully, an' Mr. Hilliard Beckwith, as de missus married
all of 'em. Dar wuz twenty-one other slaves, an' we got
beat ever' onct in a while.

"When dey told us dat de Yankees wuz comin' we wuz
also told dat iffen we didn't behave dat we'd be shot; an'
we believed it. We would'uv behaved anyhow, case we had
good plank houses, good food, an' shoes. We had Saturday
an' Sunday off an' we wuz happy.

"De missus, she raised de nigger babies so's de
mammies could wuck. I 'members de times when she rock me
ter sleep an' put me ter bed in her own bed. I wuz happy
den as I thinks back of it, until dem Yankees come.

"Dey come on a Chuesday; an' dey started by
burnin' de cotton house an' killin' most of de chickens an'
pigs. Way atter awhile dey fin's de cellar an' dey drinks

brandy till dey gits wobbly in de legs. Atter dat dey
comes up on de front porch an' calls my missus. When she
comes ter de do' dey tells her dat dey am goin' in de house
ter look things over. My missus dejicts, case ole marster
am away at de war, but dat doan do no good. Dey cusses her
scan'lous an' dey dares her ter speak. Dey robs de house,
takin' dere knives an' splittin' mattresses, pillows an'
ever' thing open lookin' fer valerables, an' ole missus
dasen't open her mouth.

"Dey camped dar in de grove fer two days, de
officers takin' de house an' missus leavin' home an' goin'
ter de neighbor's house. Dey make me stay dar in de house
wid 'em ter tote dere brandy frum de cellar, an' ter make
'em some mint jelup. Well, on de secon' night dar come de
wust storm I'se eber seed. De lightnin' flash, de thrunder
roll, an' de house shook an' rattle lak a earthquake had
struck it.

"Dem Yankees warn't supposed ter be superstitious,
but lemmie tell yo', dey wuz some skeered dat night; an'
I hyard a Captain say dat de witches wuz abroad. Atter
awhile lightnin' struck de Catawba tree dar at de side of
de house an' de soldiers camped round about dat way marched
off ter de barns, slave cabins an' other places whar dey

wuz safter dan at dat place. De next mornin' dem Yankees moved frum dar an' dey ain't come back fer nothin'.

"We wuzn't happy at de surrender an' we cussed ole Abraham Lincoln all ober de place. We wuz told de disadvantages of not havin' no edercation, but shucks, we doan need no book larnin' wid ole marster ter look atter us.

"My mammy an' pappy stayed on dar de rest of dere lives, an' I stayed till I wuz sixteen. De Ku Klux Klan got atter me den 'bout fightin' wid a white boy. Dat night I slipped in de woods an' de nex' day I went ter Raleigh. I got a job dar an' eber' since den I'se wucked fer myself, but now I can't wuck an' I wish dat yo' would apply fer my ole aged pension fer me.

"I went back ter de ole plantation long as my pappy, mammy, an' de marster an' missus lived. Sometimes, when I gits de chanct I goes back now. Course now de slave cabins am gone, ever' body am dead, an' dar ain't nothin' familiar 'cept de bent Catawba tree; but it 'minds me of de happy days."

AC

N. C. District <u>No. 2</u>   Subject <u>JOHN C. BECTOM</u>

Worker <u>T. Pat Matthews</u>   Story teller <u>John C. Bectom</u>

No. Words <u>1,566</u>   Editor <u>Daisy Bailey Waitt</u>

JOHN C. BECTOM

"My name is John C. Bectom. I was born Oct. 7,
1862, near Fayetteville, Cumberland County, North Carolina.
My father's name was Simon Bectom. He was 86 years of age
when he died. He died in 1910 at Fayetteville, N. C. My
mother's name was Harriet Bectom. She died in 1907, May
23, when she was seventy years old. My brother's were
named Ed, Kato and Willie. I was third of the boys. My
sisters were Lucy, Anne and Alice. My father first belonged
to Robert Wooten of Craven County, N. C. Then he was sold
by the Wootens to the Bectoms of Wayne County, near Goldsboro,
the county seat. My mother first belonged to the McNeills
of Cumberland County. Miss Mary McNeill married a McFadden,
and her parents gave my mother to Mis' Mary. Mis' Mary's
daughter in time married Ezekial King and my mother was then
given to her by Mis' Mary McFadden, her mother. Mis' Lizzie
McFadden became a King. My grandmother was named Lucy
Murphy. She belonged to the Murpheys. All the slaves were
given off to the children of the family as they married.

"My father and mother told me stories of how they
were treated at different places. When my grandmother was
with the Murpheys they would make her get up, and begin

burning logs in new grounds before daybreak. They also made her plow, the same as any of the men on the plantation. They plowed till dusk-dark before they left the fields to come to the house. They were not allowed to attend any dances or parties unless they slipped off unknowin's. They had candy pullings sometimes too. While they would be there the patterollers would visit them. Sometimes the patterollers whipped all they caught at this place, all they set their hands on, unless they had a pass.

"They fed us mighty good. The food was well cooked. They gave the slaves an acre of ground to plant and they could sell the crop and have the money. The work on this acre was done on moonshiny nights and holidays. Sometimes slaves would steal the marster's chickens or a hog and slip off to another plantation and have it cooked. We had plenty of clothes, and one pair o' shoes a year. You had to take care of them because you only got one pair a year. They were given at Christmas every year. The clothes were made on the plantation.

"There were corn mills on the plantation, and rice mills, and threshing machines. The plantation had about 300 acres in farm land. The enclosure was three miles.

My marster lived in a fine house. It took a year to build
it. There were about 16 rooms in it. We slaves called it
the great house. Some of the slaves ran away and finally
reached Ohio. There was no jail on the plantation. Sometimes the overseer would whip us.

"The Kings had no overseers. King beat his slaves
with a stick. I remember seeing him do this as well as I
can see that house over there. He became blind. An owl
scratched him in the face when he was trying to catch him,
and his face got into sich a fix he went to Philadelphia
for treatment, but they could not cure him. He finally
went blind. I have seen him beat his slaves after he was
blind. I remember it well. He beat 'em with a stick. He
was the most sensitive man you ever seed. He ran a store.
After he was blind you could han' him a piece of money and
he could tell you what it was.

"There were no churches on the plantation but
prayer meeting' were held in the quarters. Slaves were
not allowed to go to the white folk's church unless they
were coach drivers, etc. No sir, not in that community.
They taught the slaves the Bible. The children of the
marster would go to private school. We small Negro children
looked after the babies in the cradles and other young

children. When the white children studied their lessons
I studied with them. When they wrote in the sand I wrote
in the sand too. The white children, and not the marster
or mistress, is where I got started in learnin' to read
and write.

"We had corn shuckings, candy pullings, dances,
prayer meetings. We went to camp meetin' on Camp Meeting
days in August when the crops were laid by. We played
games of high jump, jumping over the pole held by two
people, wrestling, leap frog, and jumping. We sang the
songs, 'Go tell Aunt Patsy'. 'Some folks says a nigger
wont steal, I caught six in my corn field' 'Run nigger
run, the patteroller ketch you, Run nigger run like you
did the other day'.

"When slaves got sick marster looked after them.
He gave them blue mass and casteroil. Dr. McDuffy also
treated us. Dr. McSwain vaccinated us for small pox.
My sister died with it. When the slaves died marster
buried them. They dug a grave with a tomb in it. I do
not see any of them now. The slaves were buried in a
plain box.

"The marsters married the slaves without any
papers. All they did was to say perhaps to Jane and Frank,

'Frank, I pronounce you and Jane man and wife.' But the
woman did not take the name of her husband, she kept the
name of the family who owned her.

"I remember seeing the Yankees near Fayetteville.
They shot a bomb shell at Wheeler's Calvary, and it hit
near me and buried in the ground. Wheeler's Calvary came
first and ramsaked the place. They got all the valuables
they could, andburned the bridge, the covered bridge over
Cape Fear river, but when the Yankees got there they had
a pontoon bridge to cross on,--all those provision wagons
and such. When they passed our place it was in the morning.
They nearly scared me to death. They passed right by our
door, Sherman's army. They began passing, so the white
folks said, at 9 o'clock in the mornin'. At 9 o'clock at
night they were passin' our door on foot. They said there
were two hundred and fifty thousan' o' them passed. Some
camped in my marster's old fiel'. A Yankee caught one of
my marster's shoats and cut off one of the hind quarters,
gave it to me, and told me to carry and give it to my
mother. I was so small I could not tote it, so I drug
it to her. I called her when I got in hollering distance
of the house and she came and got it. The Yankees called
us Johnnie, Dinah, Bill and other funny names. They beat

their drums and sang songs. One of the Yankees sang 'Rock
a Bye Baby'. At that time Jeff Davis money was plentiful.
My mother had about $1000. It was so plentiful it was
called Jeff Davis shucks. My mother had bought a pair of
shoes, and had put them in a chest. A Yankee came and took
the shoes and wore them off, leaving his in their place.
They tol' us we were free. Sometimes the marster would
get cruel to the slaves if they acted like they were free.

"Mat Holmes, a slave, was wearing a ball and chain
as a punishment for running away. Marster Ezekial King
put it on him. He has slept in the bed with me, wearing
that ball and chain. The cuff had imbedded in his leg,
it was swollen so. This was right after the Yankees came
through. It was March, the 9th of March, when the Yankees
came through. Mat Holmes had run away with the ball and
chain on him and was in the woods then. He hid out staying
with us at night until August. Then my mother took him to
the Yankee garrison at Fayetteville. A Yankee officer
then took him to a black smith shop and had the ball and
chain cut off his leg. The marsters would tell the slaves
to go to work that they were not free, that they still
belonged to them, but one would drop out and leave, then
another. There was little work done on the farm, and

finally most of the slaves learned they were free.

"Abraham Lincoln was one of the greatest men that
ever lived. He was the cause of us slaves being free.
No doubt about that. I didn't think anything of Jeff
Davis. He tried to keep us in slavery. I think slavery
was an injustice, not right. Our privilege is to live
right, and live according to the teachings of the Bible,
to treat our fellowman right. To do this I feel we should
belong to some religious organization and live as near
right as we know how.

"The overseers and patterollers in the time of
slavery were called poor white trash by the slaves.

"On the plantations not every one, but some of
the slave holders would have some certain slave women
reserved for their own use. Sometimes children almost
white would be born to them. I have seen many of these
children. Sometimes the child would be said to belong to
the overseer, and sometimes it would be said to belong to
the marster.

AC

N. C. District <u>No. 2</u>   Subject <u>AUNT LAURA</u>

Worker <u>Mary A. Hicks</u>   Story teller <u>LAURA BELL</u>

No. Words <u>610</u>   Editor <u>Geo. L. Andrews</u>

AUNT LAURA

An interview with Laura Bell, 73 years old, of 2 Bragg
Street, Raleigh, North Carolina.

Being informed that Laura Bell was an old slavery
Negro, I went immediately to the little two-room shack
with its fallen roof and shaky steps. As I approached the
shack I noticed that the storm had done great damage to
the chaney-berry tree in her yard, fallen limbs litterin'
the ground, which was an inch deep in garbage and water.

The porch was littered with old planks and huge tubs
and barrels of stagnant water. There was only room for one
chair and in that sat a tall Negro woman clad in burlap
bags and in her lap she held a small white flea-bitten dog
which growled meaningly.

When I reached the gate, which swings on one rusty
hinge, she bade me come in and the Carolina Power and
Light Company men, who were at work nearby, laughed as I
climbed over the limbs and garbage and finally found room
for one foot on the porch and one on the ground.

"I wus borned in Mount Airy de year 'fore de Yankees
come, bein' de fourth of five chilluns. My mammy an' daddy
Minerva Jane an' Wesley 'longed ter Mr. Mack Strickland an'
we lived on his big place near Mount Airy.

"Mr. Mack wus good ter us, dey said. He give us enough ter eat an' plenty of time ter weave clothes fer us ter wear. I've hearn mammy tell of de corn shuckin's an' dances dey had an' 'bout some whuppin's too.

"Marse Mack's overseer, I doan know his name, wus gwine ter whup my mammy onct, an' pappy do' he ain't neber make no love ter mammy comes up an' takes de whuppin' fer her. Atter dat dey cou'ts on Sadday an' Sunday an' at all de sociables till dey gits married.

"I'se hearn her tell 'bout how he axed Marse Mack iffen he could cou't mammy an' atter Marse Mack sez he can he axes her ter marry him.

"She tells him dat she will an' he had 'em married by de preacher de nex' time he comes through dat country.

"I growed up on de farm an' when I wus twelve years old I met Thomas Bell. My folks said dat I wus too young fer ter keep company so I had ter meet him 'roun' an' about fer seberal years, I think till I wus fifteen.

"He axed me ter marry him while he wus down on de creek bank a fishin' an' I tol' him yes, but when he starts ter kiss me I tells him dat der's many a slip twixt de cup an' de lip an' so he has ter wait till we gits married.

"We runned away de nex' Sadday an' wus married by a Justice of de Peace in Mount Airy.

"Love ain't what hit uster be by a long shot," de ole woman reflected, "'Cause dar ain't many folks what loves all de time. We moved ter Raleigh forty years ago, an' Tom has been daid seberal years now. We had jest one chile but hit wus borned daid.

"Chilluns ain't raised ter be clean lak we wus. I knows dat de house ain't so clean but I doan feel so much lak doin' nothin', I jest went on a visit 'bout seben blocks up de street dis mo'nin' an' so I doan feel lak cleanin' up none."

I cut the interview short thereby missing more facts, as the odor was anything but pleasant and I was getting tired of standing in that one little spot.

"Thank you for comin'", she called, and her dog growled again.

N. C. District No. 2   Subject EMMA BLALOCK

Worker T. Pat Matthews   Story teller Emma Blalock

No. Words   1153   Editor Geo. L. Andrews

EMMA BLALOCK
88 years old
529 Bannon Avenue
Raleigh, N. C.

"I shore do 'member de Yankees wid dere blue uniforms wid brass buttons on 'em. I wus too small to work any but I played in de yard wid my oldes' sister, Katie. She is dead long ago. My mother belonged to ole man John Griffith an' I belonged to him. His plantation wus down here at Auburn in Wake County. My father wus named Edmund Rand. He belonged to Mr. Nat Rand. He lived in Auburn. De plantations wus not fur apart. Dere wus about twenty-five slaves on de plantation whur mother an' me stayed.

"Marse John used ter take me on his knee an' sing, 'Here is de hammer, Shing ding. Gimme de Hammer, shing ding.' Marster loved de nigger chilluns on his plantation. When de war ended father come an' lived with us at Marse John's plantation. Marster John Griffith named me Emmy. My grandfather on my fathers side wus named Harden Rand, an' grandmother wus named Mason Rand. My grandfather on my mother's side wus named Antny Griffiths an' grandmother wus named Nellie.

"Our food wus a plenty and well cooked. Marster
fed his niggers good. We had plenty of homespun dresses
and we got shoes once a year, at Christmas Eve. I ken
'member it just as good. We got Christmas Holidays an'
a stockin' full of candy an' peanuts. Sometimes we got
ginger snaps at Christmas. My grandmother cooked 'em.
She wus a good cook. My mother's missus wus Miss Jetsy
Griffith and my father's missus wus Lucy Rand. Dey wus
both mighty good women. You know I am ole. I ken 'member
all dem good white folks. Dey give us Fourth July Holidays.
Dey come to town on dat day. Dey wore, let me tell you
what dey wore, dey wore dotted waist blouses an' white
pants. Dat wus a big day to ever'body, de Fourth of July.
Dey begun singing at Auburn an' sung till dey reached
Raleigh. Auburn is nine miles from Raleigh. Dere wus a
lot of lemonade. Dey made light bread in big ovens an'
had cheese to eat wid it. Some said just goin' on de fofe
to git lemonade an' cheese.

"In the winter we had a lot of possums to eat an'
a lot of rabbits too. At Christmas time de men hunted
and caught plenty game. We barbecued it before de fire.
I 'members seein' mother an' grandmother swinging rabbits

'fore de fire to cook 'em. Dey would turn an' turn 'em
till dey wus done. Dey hung some up in de chimbly an'
dry 'em out an' keep 'em a long time an' dat is de reason
I won't eat a rabbit toady. No Sir! I won't eat a
rabbit. I seed 'em mess wid 'em so much turned me 'ginst
eatin' 'em.

"I don't know how much lan' Marster John owned but,
Honey, dat wus some plantation. It reached from Auburn
to de Neuse River. Yes Sir, it did, 'cause I been down
dere in corn hillin' time an' we fished at twelve o'clock
in Neuse River. Marster John had overseers. Dere wus
six of 'em. Dey rode horses over de fields but I don't
'member dere names.

"I never seen a slave whupped but dey wus whupped
on de plantation an' I heard de grown folks talkin' 'bout
it. My uncles Nat an' Bert Griffiths wus both whupped.
Uncle Nat would not obey his missus rules an' she had him
whupped. Dey whupped Uncle Bert 'cause he stayed drunk
so much. He loved his licker an' he got drunk an' cut
up bad, den dey whupped him. You could git plenty whiskey
den. Twon't like it is now. No sir, it won't. Whiskey
sold fur ten cents a quart. Most ever' body drank it but

you hardly ever seed a man drunk. Slaves wus not whupped for drinkin'. Dere Marsters give 'em whiskey but dey wus whupped for gittin' drunk. (Dere wus a jail, a kind of stockade built of logs, on de farm to put slaves in when dey wouldn't mind.) I never say any slave put on de block an' sold, but I saw Aunt Helen Rand cryin' because her Marster Nat Rand sold her boy, Fab Rand.

"No Sir, no readin' an' writin'. You had to work. Ha! ha! You let your marster or missus ketch you wid a book. Dat wus a strict rule dat no learnin' wus to be teached. I can't read an' write. (If it wus not fur my mother wit don't know what would become of me.) We had prayer meetings around at de slave houses. I 'member it well. We turned down pots on de inside of de house at de door to keep marster an' missus from hearin' de singin' an' prayin'. Marster an' his family lived in de great house an' de slave quarters wus 'bout two hundred yards away to the back of de great house. Dey wus arranged in rows. When de war ended we all stayed on wid de families Griffiths an' Rands till dey died, dat is all 'cept my father an' me. He lef' an' I lef'. I been in Raleigh forty-five years. I married Mack Blalock in Raleigh. He been dead seven years.

"My mother had two boys, Antny an' Wesley. She
had four girls, Katie, Grissie, Mary Ella an' Emma. I
had three chilluns, two are livin' yet. They both live
in Raleigh.

"We had big suppers an' dinners at log rollin's -
an' corn shuckin's in slavery time ha! ha! plenty of
corn licker for ever'body, both white an' black. Ever'-
body helped himself. Dr. Tom Busbee, one good ole white
man, looked after us when we got sick, an' he could make
you well purty quick, 'cause he wus good an' 'cause he
wus sorry fer you. He wus a feelin' man. Course we took
erbs. I tell you what I took. Scurrey grass, chana balls
dey wus for worms. Scurrey grass worked you out. Dey
give us winter green to clense our blood. We slaves an'
a lot of de white folks drank sassafras tea in de place
of coffee. We sweetened it wid brown sugar, honey, or
molasses, just what we had in dat line. I think slavery
wus a right good thing. Plenty to eat an' wear.

"When you gits a tooth pulled now it costs two
dollars, don't it? Well in slavery time I had a tooth
botherin' me. My mother say, Emma, take dis egg an' go
down to Doctor Busbee an' give it to him an' git your

tooth pulled. I give him one egg. He took it an' pulled
my tooth. Try dat now, if you wants to an' see what
happens. Yes, slavery wus a purty good thing."

N. C. District <u>No. 2</u>   Subject <u>Days on the Plantation</u>

Worker <u>Mary A. Hicks</u>   Person Interviewed <u>Uncle David Blount</u>

No. Words <u>1430</u>   Editor <u>Daisy Bailey Waitt</u>

DAYS ON THE PLANTATION

As told by Uncle David Blount, formerly of Beaufort
County, who did not know his age. "De Marster," he
refers to was Major Wm. A. Blount, who owned plantations
in several parts of North Carolina.

"Yes mam, de days on de plantation wuz de happy days.
De marster made us wuck through de week but on Sadays we
uster go swimmin' in de riber an' do a lot of other things
dat we lak ter do.

"We didn't mind de wuck so much case de ground wuz
soft as ashes an' de marster let us stop and rest when we
got tired. We planted 'taters in de uplan's and co'n in
ie lowgroun's nex' de riber. It wuz on de Cape Fear an'
on hot days when we wuz a-pullin' de fodder we'd all stop
wuck 'bout three o'clock in de ebenin' an' go swimmin'.
Atter we come out'n de water we would wuck harder dan
eber an' de marster wuz good to us, case we did wuck an'
we done what he ast us.

"I 'members onct de marster had a oberseer dar dat
wuz meaner dan a mean nigger. He always hired good oberseers an' a whole lot of times he let some Negro slave
obersee. Well, dis oberseer beat some of de half grown
boys till de blood run down ter dar heels an' he tole de
rest of us dat if we told on him dat he'd kill us. We
don't dasen't ast de marster ter git rid of de man so dis
went on fer a long time.

"It wuz cold as de debil one day an' dis oberseer
had a gang of us a-clearin' new groun'. One boy ast if
he could warm by de bresh heap. De oberseer said no,and
atter awhile de boy had a chill. De oberseer don't care,
but dat night de boy am a sick nigger. De nex' mornin'
de marster gits de doctor,an' de doctor say dat de boy
has got pneumonia. He tells 'em ter take off de boys
shirt an' grease him wid some tar, turpentine,an! ker-
osene,an' when dey starts ter take de shirt off dey fin's
dat it am stuck.

"Dey had ter grease de shirt ter git it off case de
blood whar de oberseer beat him had stuck de shirt tight
ter de skin. De marster wuz in de room an' he axed de
boy how come it, an' de boy tole him.

"De marster sorta turns white an' he says ter me,
'Will yo' go an' ast de oberseer ter stop hyar a minute,
please?'

"When de oberseer comes up de steps he axes sorta
sassy-like, 'What yo' want?'

"De marster says, 'Pack yo' things an' git off'n
my place as fast as yo' can, yo' pesky varmit.'

"De oberseer sasses de marster some more,an' den I
sees de marster fairly loose his temper for de first time.
He don't say a word but he walks ober, grabs de oberseer
by de shoulder, sets his boot right hard 'ginst de seat
of his pants an' sen's him, all drawed up, out in de yard

on his face. He close up lak a umbrella for a minute den
he pulls hisself all tergether an' he limps out'n dat yard
an' we ain't neber seed him no more.

"No mam, dar wuzent no marryin' on de plantation dem
days, an' as one ole 'oman raised all of de chilluns me
an' my brother Johnnie ain't neber knowed who our folkses
wuz. Johnnie wuz a little feller when de war ended, but
I wuz in most of de things dat happen on de plantation
fer a good while.

"One time dar, I done fergit de year, some white mens
comes down de riber on a boat an' dey comes inter de fiel's
an' talks ter a gang of us an' dey says dat our masters
ain't treatin' us right. Dey tells us dat we orter be
paid fer our wuck, an' dat we hadn't ort ter hab passes ter
go anywhar. Dey also tells us dat we ort ter be allowed
ter tote guns if we wants 'em. Dey says too dat sometime
our marsters was gwine ter kill us all.

"I laughs at 'em, but some of dem fool niggers list-
ens ter 'em an' it 'pears dat dese men gib de niggers some
guns atter I left an' promised ter bring 'em some more
de nex' week.

"I fin's out de nex' day 'bout dis an' I goes an'
tells de marster. He sorta laughs an' scratches his head,
'Dem niggers am headed fer trouble, Dave,'he says ter me,
'an I wants yo' ter help me.'

"I says, 'Yas sar, marster.'

"An' he goes on, 'Yo' fin's out when de rest of de

guns comes Dave,an" let me know.'

"When de men brings back de guns I tells de marster,
an' I also tells him dat dey wants ter hold er meetin'.

"'All right,' he says an' laughs, 'dey can have de
meetin'. Yo' tell 'em, Dave,dat I said dat dey can meet
on Chuesday night in de pack house.'

"Chuesday ebenin' he sen's dem all off to de low
groun's but me,an' he tells me ter nail up de shutters
ter de pack house an' ter nail 'em up good.

"I does lak he tells me ter do an' dat night de
niggers marches in an' sneaks dar guns in too. I is
lyin' up in de loft an' I hyars dem say dat atter de meetin' dey is gwine ter go up ter de big house an' kill de
whole fambly.

"I gits out of de winder an' I runs ter de house an
tells de marster. Den me an' him an' de young marster goes
out an' quick as lightnin', I slams de pack house door an'
I locks it. Den de marster yells at dem, 'I'se got men an'
guns out hyar, 'he yells, 'an' if yo' doan throw dem guns
out of de hole up dar in de loft, an' throw dem ebery one
out I'se gwine ter stick fire ter dat pack house.'

"De niggers 'liberates for a few minutes an' den
dey throws de guns out. I knows how many dey has got so
I counts till dey throw dem all out, den I gathers up dem

guns an' I totes 'em off ter de big house.

"Well sar, we keeps dem niggers shet up fer about a week on short rations; an' at de end of dat time dem niggers am kyored for good. When dey comes out dey had three oberseers 'stid of one, an' de rules am stricter dan eber before, an' den de marster goes off ter de war.

"I reckon I was 'bout fifteen or sixteen den; an' de marster car's me 'long fer his pusonal sarvant an' body guard an' he leabes de rest of dem niggers in de fiel's ter wuck like de dickens while I laughs at dem Yankees.

"Jim belonged to Mr. Harley who lived in New Hanover County during de war, in fac' he was young Massa Harley's slave; so when young Massa Tom went to de war Jim went along too.

"Dey wuz at Manassas, dey tells me, when Massa Tom got kilt, and de orders wuz not to take no bodies off de field right den.

"Course ole massa down near Wilmington, doan know 'bout young Massa Tom, but one night dey hears Jim holler at de gate. Dey goes runnin' out an' Jim has brung Massa Tom's body all dat long ways home so dat he can be buried in de family burian ground.

"De massa frees Jim dat night; but he stays on a long time atter de war, an' tell de day he died he hated

de Yankees for killing Massa Tom.   In fact we all hated de
Yankees, 'specially atter we near 'bout starve dat first
winter.   I tried ter make a libin' fer me an' Johnnie but
it was bad goin'; den I comes ter Raleigh an' I gits 'long
better.   Atter I gits settled I brings Johnnie, an' so we
done putty good.

"Dat's all I can tell yo' now Miss, but if'n yo'll
come back sometime I'll tell yo' de rest of de tales."

Shortly after the above interview Uncle Dave who
was failing fast was taken to the County Home, where he
died.   He was buried on May 4th, 1937, the rest of the tale
remaining untold.

N. C. District No. 2   Subject Ex-Slave Story

Worker Mary A. Hicks   Person Interviewed Clay Bobbit

No. Words 459   Editor Daisy Bailey Waitt

EX-SLAVE STORY

An interview with Clay Bobbit, 100 of S. Harrington
Street, Raleigh, N. C., May 27, 1937;

"I wuz borned May 2, 1837 in Warren County to
Washington an' Delisia Bobbit.. Our Marster wuz named
Richard Bobbit, but we all calls him Massa Dick.

"Massa Dick ain't good ter us, an' on my arm hyar,
jist above de elbow am a big scar dis day whar he whupped
me wid a cowhide. He ain't whupped me fer nothin' 'cept
dat I is a nigger. I had a whole heap of dem whuppin's,
mostly case I won't obey his orders an' I'se seed slaves
beat 'most ter deff.

"I wuz married onct 'fore de war by de broom stick
ceremony, lak all de rest of de slaves wuz but shucks
dey sold away my wife 'fore we'd been married a year an'
den de war come on.

"I had one brother, Henry who am wuckin' fer
de city, an' one sister what wuz named Deliah. She
been daid dese many years now.

"Massa Dick owned a powerful big plantation an'
ober a hundert slaves, an' we wucked on short rations
an' went nigh naked. We ain't gone swimmin' ner huntin'

ner nothin' an' we ain't had no pleasures 'less we runs
away ter habe 'em. Eben when we sings we had ter turn
down a pot in front of de do' ter ketch de noise.

"I knowed some pore white trash; our oberseer wuz
one, an' de shim shams[1] wuz also nigh 'bout also. We ain't
had no use fer none of 'em an ' we shorely ain't carin'
whe'her dey has no use fer us er not.

"De Ku Kluxes ain't done nothin' fer us case dar ain't
many in our neighborhood. Yo' see de Yankees ain't come
through dar, an' we is skeerd of dem anyhow. De white folks
said dat de Yankees would kill us if'en dey ketched us.

"I ain't knowed nothin' 'bout de Yankees, ner de surrender so I stays on fer seberal months atter de wahr wuz ober,
den I comes ter Raleigh an' goes ter wuck fer de city. I
wucks fer de city fer nigh on fifty years, I reckon, an'
jis' lately I retired.

"I'se been sick fer 'bout four months an' on de second
day of May. De day when I wuz a hundert years old I warn't
able ter git ter de city lot, but I got a lot uv presents.

"Dis 'oman am my third lawful wife. I married her
three years ago."[2]

1. Shim Sham, Free Issues or Negroes of mixed blood.
2. The old man was too ill to walk out on the porch for
   his picture, and his mind wandered too much to give a
   connected account of his life.

N.C. District_# 2_____   Subject: Ex-Slave Story____

No. Words:___793_____   Story Teller:Henry Bobbitt__

Worker: Mary A. Hicks____   Editor: Daisy Bailey Waitt__

EX-SLAVE STORIES

An interview with Henry Bobbitt, 87 of Raleigh,
Wake County N.C. May 13, 1937 by Mary A. Hicks.

"I wuz borned at Warrenton in Warren County in
1850. My father wuz named Washington, atter General
Washington an' my mamma wuz named Diasia atter a woman
in a story. Us an' 'bout forty or fifty other slaves
belonged ter Mr. Richard Bobbitt an' we wucked his four
hundred acres o' land fer him. I jist had one brother
named Clay, atter Henry Clay, which shows how Massa Dick
voted, an' Delilah, which shows dat ole missus read de
Bible.

"We farmed, makin' tobacco,cotton, co'n, wheat
an' taters. Massa Dick had a whole passel o' fine horses
an' our Sunday job wuz ter take care of 'em, an' clean up
round de house. Yes mam, we wucked seben days a week, from
sunup till sundown six days,an' from seben till three or
four on a Sunday.

"We didn't have many tear-downs an' prayer meetin's
an' sich, case de fuss sturbed ole missus who wuz kinder
sickly. When we did have sompin' we turned down a big
washpot in front of de do', an' it took up de fuss, an'
folkses in de yard can't hyar de fuss. De patterollers

would git you iffen you went offen de premises widout a
pass, an' dey said dat dey would beat you scandelous. I
seed a feller dat dey beat onct an' he had scars as big as
my fingers all ober his body.

"I got one whuppin' dat I 'members, an' dat wuz jist
a middlin' one. De massa told me ter pick de cotton an' I
sot down in de middle an' didn't wuck a speck. De oberseer
come an' he frailed me wid a cotton-stalk; he wuz a heap
meaner ter de niggers dan Massa Dick wuz. I saw some niggers
what wuz beat bad, but I ain't neber had no bad beatin'.

"We libed in log houses wid sand floors an' stick an'
dirt chimneys an' we warn't 'lowed ter have no gyarden, ner
chickens, ner pigs. We ain't had no way o' makin' money an'
de fun wuz only middlin'. We had ter steal what rabbits we
et from somebody elses boxes on some udder plantation, case
de massa won't let us have none o' our own, an' we ain't had
no time ter hunt ner fish.

"Now talkin' 'bout sompin' dat we'd git a whuppin' fer,
dat wuz fer havin' a pencil an' a piece of paper er a slate.
Iffen you jist looked lak you wanted ter larn ter read er
write you got a lickin'.

"Dar wuz two colored women lived nigh us an' dey wuz
called "free issues," but dey wuz really witches. I ain't
really seen 'em do nothin' but I hyard a whole lot

'bout 'em puttin' spells on folkses an' I seed tracks whar
dey had rid Massa Dick's hosses an' eber mo'nin' de hosses
manes an' tails would be all twisted an' knotted up. I know
dat dey done dat case I seed it wid my own eyes. Dey doctored
lots of people an' our folkses ain't neber had no doctor fer
nothin' dat happen.

"You wuz axin' 'bout de slave sales, an' I want ter
tell you dat I has seen some real sales an' I'se seed niggers,
whole bunches of 'em, gwin' ter Richmond ter be sold. Dey
wuz mostly chained, case dey wuz new ter de boss, an' he
doan know what ter 'spect. I'se seed some real sales in
Warrenton too, an' de mammies would be sold from deir chilluns
an' dare would be a whole heap o' cryin' an' mou'nin' 'bout
hit. I tell you folkses ain't lak dey uster be, 'specially
niggers. Uster be when a nigger cries he whoops an' groans an'
hollers an' his whole body rocks, an' dat am de way dey done
sometime at de sales.

"Speakin' 'bout haints: I'se seed a whole lot o' things,
, but de worst dat eber happen wuz 'bout twenty years ago
when a han'ts hand hit me side o' de haid. I bet dat hand
weighed a hundred pounds an' it wuz as cold as ice. I ain't
been able ter wuck fer seben days an' nights an' I still can't
turn my haid far ter de left as you sees.

"I reckon 'bout de funniest thing 'bout our planta-

tion wuz de marryin'. A couple got married by sayin' dat
dey wuz, but it couldn't last fer longer dan five years.
Dat wuz so iffen one of 'em got too weakly ter have chilluns
de other one could git him another wife or husban'.

"I 'members de day moughty well when de Yankees
come. Massa Dick he walked de floor an' cussed Sherman fer
takin' his niggers away. All o' de niggers lef', of course,
an' me, I walked clean ter Raleigh ter find out if I wuz
really free, an' I couldn't unnerstan' half of it.

"Well de first year I slept in folkses woodhouses an'
barns an' in de woods or any whar else I could find. I wucked
hyar an' dar, but de folkses' jist give me sompin' ter eat
an' my clothes wuz in strings 'fore de spring o' de year.

"Yo' axes me what I thinks of Massa Lincoln? Well, I
thinks dat he wuz doin' de wust thing dat he could ter turn
all dem fool niggers loose when dey ain't got no place ter go
an' nothin' ter eat. Who helped us out den? Hit wuzn't de
Yankees, hit wuz de white folkses what wuz left wid deir craps
in de fiel's, an' wuz robbed by dem Yankees, ter boot. My ole
massa, fur instance, wuz robbed uv his fine hosses an' his
feed stuff an' all dem kaigs o' liquor what he done make hisself, sides his money an' silver.

"Slavery wuz a good thing den, but de world jist got
better an' outgrowed it."

EH

N. C. District **No. 2**   Subject **HERNDON BOGAN**

Worker **Mary A. Hicks**   Story teller **Herndon Bogan**

No. Words **863**   Editor **Daisy Bailey Waitt**

HERNDON BOGAN

Ex - Slave Story

An interview with Herndon Bogan, 76 (?) of State
Prison, Raleigh, N. C.

"I wus bawned in Union County, South Carolina on
de plantation o' Doctor Bogan, who owned both my mammy
Issia, an' my pap Edwin. Dar wus six o' us chilluns,
Clara, Lula, Joe, Tux, Mack an' me.

"I doan 'member much 'bout slavery days 'cept dat
my white folkses wus good ter us. Dar wus a heap o'
slaves, maybe a hundert an' fifty. I 'members dat we
wucked hard, but we had plenty ter eat an' w'ar, eben iffen
we did w'ar wood shoes.

"I kin barely recolleck 'fore de war dat I'se seed
a heap o' cocks fightin' in pits an' a heap o' horse
racin'. When de marster winned he 'ud give us niggers
a big dinner or a dance, but if he lost, oh!

"My daddy wus gived ter de doctor when de doctor
wus married an' dey shore loved each other. One day
marster, he comes in an' he sez dat de Yankees am aimin'
ter try ter take his niggers way from him, but dat dey
am gwine ter ketch hell while dey does hit. When he

sez dat he starts ter walkin' de flo'. 'I'se gwine ter
leave yore missus in yore keer, Edwin,' he sez.

"But pa 'lows, 'Wid all respec' fer yore wife sar,
she am a Yankee too, an' I'd ruther go wid you ter de war.
Please sar, massa, let me go wid you ter fight dem Yanks.'

"At fust massa 'fuses, den he sez, 'All right.' So
off dey goes ter de war, massa on a big hoss, an' my pap
on a strong mule 'long wid de blankets an' things.

"Dey tells me dat ole massa got shot one night, an'
dat pap grabs de gun 'fore hit hits de earth an' lets de
Yanks have hit.

"I 'members dat dem wus bad days fer South Carolina, we gived all o' de food ter de soldiers, an' missus,
eben do' she has got some Yankee folks in de war, l'arns
ter eat cabbages an' kush an' berries.

"I 'members dat on de day of de surrender, least-
ways de day dat we hyard 'bout hit, up comes a Yankee
an' axes ter see my missus. I is shakin', I is dat
skeerd, but I bucks up an' I tells him dat my missus doan
want ter see no blue coat.

"He grins, an' tells me ter skedaddle, an' 'bout den
my missus comes out an' so help me iffen she doan hug
dat dratted Yank. Atter awhile I gathers dat he's her
brother, but at fust I ain't seed no sense in her cryin'

an' sayin' 'thank God', over an' over.

"Well sar, de massa an' pap what had gone off mad an' healthy an' ridin' fine beastes comes back walkin' an' dey looked sick. Massa am white as cotton, an' so help me, iffen my pap, who wus black as sin, ain't pale too.

"Atter a few years I goes ter wuck in Spartanburg as a houseboy, den I gits a job wid de Southern Railroad an' I goes ter Charlotte ter nightwatch de tracks.

"I stays dar eighteen years, but one night I kills a white hobo who am tryin' ter rob me o' my gol' watch an' chain, an' dey gives me eighteen months. I'se been hyar six already. He wus a white man, an' jist a boy, an' I is sorry, but I comes hyar anyhow.

"I hyard a ole 'oman in Charlotte tell onct 'bout witchin' in slavery times, dar in Mecklenburg County. She wus roun' ninety, so I reckon she knows. She said dat iffen anybody wanted ter be a witch he would draw a circle on de groun' jist at de aidge o' dark an' git in de circle an' squat down.

"Dar he had ter set an' talk ter de debil, an' he mus' say, 'I will have nothin' ter do wid 'ligion, an' I wants you ter make me a witch.' Atter day he mus' bile a black cat, a bat an' a bunch of herbs an' drink de soup, den he wuz really a witch.

"When you wanted ter witch somebody, she said dat
you could take dat stuff, jist a little bit of hit an'
put hit under dat puson's doorsteps an' dey'd be sick.

"You could go thru' de key hole or down de chimney
or through de chinks in a log house, an' you could ride
a puson jist lak ridin' a hoss. Dat puson can keep you
outen his house by layin' de broom 'fore de do' an'
puttin' a pin cushion full of pins side of de bed do',
iffen he's a mind to.

"Dat puson can kill you too, by drawin' yore pitcher
an' shootin' hit in de haid or de heart too.

"Dar's a heap o' ways ter tell fortunes dat she done
tol' me but I'se done forgot now 'cept coffee groun's
an' a little of de others. You can't tell hit wid 'em
do', case hit takes knowin' how, hit shore does.

BN

N. C. District **No. 2**   Subject **ANDREW BOONE**

Worker **T. Pat Matthews**   Person Interviewed **Andrew Boone**

No. Words **1741**   Editor   **G. L. Andrews**

ANDREW BOONE
age 90 years.

Wake County, North Carolina.   Harris Farm.

"I been living in dese backer barns fifteen years.
I built this little shelter to cook under. Dey cut me
off the WPA cause dey said I wus too ole to work. Dey
tole us ole folks we need not put down our walkin'
sticks to git work cause dey jes' won't goin' to put us
on.

"Well, I had some tomatoes cooked widout any grease
for my breakfast. I had a loaf of bread yesterday, but
I et it. I ain't got any check from the ole age pension
an' I have nothin' to eat an' I am hongry. I jes' looks
to God. I set down by de road thinkin' bout how to turn
an' what to do to git a meal, when you cum along. I
thanks you fer dis dime. I guess God made you give it
to me.

"I wus glad to take you down to my livin' place to
give you my story. Dis shelter, an ole tobacco barn,
is better dan no home at all. I is a man to myself an'
I enjoy livin' out here if I could git enough to eat.

"Well de big show is coming to town. It's de
Devil's wurk. Yes sir, it's de Devil's wurk. Why dem

show folks ken make snakes an' make 'em crawl too.
Dere wus one in Watson Field in de edge of Raleigh not
long ago an' he made snakes an' made 'em crawl too.
All shows is de Devil's wurk.

"I never done anything fer myself in all my life.
I always wurked fer de Rebels. I stuck right to 'em.
Didn't have no sense fer doin' dat I guess.

"One time a Rebel saw a Yankee wid one eye, one leg
an' one arm. De Yankee wus beggin'. De Rebel went
up to him an' give him a quarter. Den he backed off
an' jes' stood a-lookin' at de Yankee, presently he went
back an' give him anudder quarter, den anudder, den
he said, 'You take dis whole dollar, you is de first
Yankee I eber seed trimmed up jes' to my notion, so take
all dis, jes' take de whole dollar, you is trimmed up to
my notion'.

"I belonged to Billy Boone in Slavery time. He wus
a preacher. He lived on an' owned a plantation in
Northampton County. The plantation wus near woodland.
The nearest river to the place wus the Roanoke. My
ole missus' name wus Nancy. When ole marster died I
stayed around wid fust one then another of the chilluns,
cause marster tole me jes' fore he died fer me to stay
wid any of 'em I wanted to stay with. All dem ole people
done dead an' gone on.

"Niggers had to go through thick an' thin in slavery
time, with rough rations most of de time, wid jes' enough
clothin' to make out wid. Our houses were built of logs
an' covered wid slabs. Dey wus rived out of blocks of
trees about 3-6 and 8ft in length. De chimleys wus
built of sticks and mud, den a coat of clay mud daubed
over 'em. De cracks in de slave houses wus daubed wid
mud too.

"We wurked from sun to sun. If we had a fire in
cold weather where we wus wurkin' marster or de overseer
would come an' put it out. We et frozen meat an'
bread many times in cold weather. After de day's wurk
in de fields wus over we had a task of pickin' de seed
from cotton till we had two ounces of lint or spin two
ounces of cotton on a spinnin' wheel. I spun cotton
on a spinnin' wheel. Dats de way people got clothes
in slavery time.

"I can't read an' write but dey learned us to count.
Dey learned us to count dis way. 'Ought is an' ought, an'
a figger is a figger, all for de white man an' nothin'
fer de nigger'. Hain't you heard people count dat way?

"Dey sold slaves jes' like people sell hosses now.
I saw a lot of slaves sold on de auction block. Dey
would strip 'em stark naked. A nigger scarred up
or whaled an' welted up wus considered a bad nigger
an' did not bring much. If his body wus not scarred,

he brought a good price. I saw a lot of slaves whupped
an' I wus whupped myself. Dey whupped me wid de cat
o' nine tails. It had nine lashes on it. Some of de
slaves wus whupped wid a cabbin paddle. Dey had forty
holes in 'em an' when you wus buckled to a barrel dey hit
your naked flesh wid de paddle an' every whur dere wus
a hole in de paddle it drawed a blister. When de whuppin'
wid de paddle wus over, dey took de cat o' nine tails an'
busted de blisters. By dis time de blood sometimes would
be runnin' down dere heels. Den de next thing wus a wash
in salt water strong enough to hold up an egg. Slaves wus
punished dat way fer runnin' away an' sich.

"If you wus out widout a pass dey would shore git
you. De paterollers shore looked after you. Dey would
come to de house at night to see who wus there. If you
wus out of place, dey would wear you out.

"Sam Joyner, a slave, belonged to marster. He wus
runnin' from de paterollers an' he fell in a ole well.
De pateroller went after marster. Marster tole 'em to
git ole Sam out an' whup him jes' as much as dey wanted
to. Dey got him out of de well an' he wus all wet an'
muddy. Sam began takin' off his shoes, den he took off
his pants an' got in his shirt tail. Marster, he say,

'What you takin' off you clothes fer Sam?' Sam, he say,
'Marster, you know you all can't whup dis nigger right over
all dese wet clothes.' Den Sam lit out. He run so fas'
he nearly flew. De paterollers got on dere hosses an'
run him but dey could not ketch him. He got away. Marster
got Sam's clothes an' carried 'em to de house. Sam slipped
up next morning put his clothes on an' marster said no
more about it.

"I wus a great big boy when de Yankees come through.
I wus drivin' a two mule team an' doin' other wurk on de
farm. I drove a two hoss wagon when dey carried slaves
to market. I went to a lot of different places.

"My marster wus a preacher, Billy Boone. He sold
an' bought niggers. He had fifty or more. He wurked
the grown niggers in two squads. My father wus named Isham
Boone and my mother wus Sarah Boone. Marster Boone whupped
wid de cabbin paddle an' de cat o' nine tails an' used
the salt bath an' dat wus 'nough. Plenty besides him
whupped dat way.

"Marster had one son, named Solomon, an' two girls,
Elsie an' Alice. My mother had four children, three boys
an' one girl. The boys were named Sam, Walter and Andrew,
dats me, an' de girl wus Cherry.

"My father had several children cause he had several
women besides mother. Mollie and Lila Lassiter, two

sisters, were also his women. Dese women wus given to
him an' no udder man wus allowed to have anything to do wid
'em. Mollie an' Lila both had chilluns by him. Dere
names wus Jim, Mollie, Liza, Rosa, Pete an' I can't
remember no more of 'em.

"De Yankees took jes' what dey wanted an' nothin'
stopped 'em, cause de surrender had come. Before de
surrender de slave owners begun to scatter de slaves
'bout from place to place to keep de Yankees from gittin'
'em. If de Yankees took a place de slaves nearby wus
moved to a place further off.

"All I done wus fer de Rebels. I wus wid 'em an'
I jes' done what I wus tole. I wus afraid of de Yankees
'cause de Rebels had told us dat de Yankees would kill us.
Dey tole us dat de Yankees would bore holes in our
shoulders an' wurk us to carts. Dey tole us we would
be treated a lot worser den dey wus treating us. Well,
de Yankees got here but they treated us fine. Den a story
went round an' round dat de marster would have to give de
slaves a mule an' a year's provisions an' some lan', about
forty acres, but dat wus not so. Dey nebber did give us
anything. When de war ended an' we wus tole we wus free,
we stayed on wid marster cause we had nothin' an' nowhere

to go.

"We moved about from farm to farm. Mother died an'
father married Maria Edwards after de surrender. He did
not live wid any of his other slave wives dat I knows of.

"I have wurked as a han' on de farm most of de time
since de surrender and daddy wurked most of de time as
a han', but he had gardens an' patches most everywhere he
wurked. I wurked in New York City for fifteen years with
Crawford and Banhay in de show business. I advertised
for 'em. I dressed in a white suit, white shirt, an'
white straw hat, and wore tan shoes. I had to be a
purty boy. I had to have my shoes shined twice a day. I
lived at 18 Manilla Lane, New York City. It is between
McDougall Street and 6th Avenue. I married Clara Taylor
in New York City. We had two children. The oldest one
lives in New York. The other died an' is buried in
Raleigh.

"In slavery time they kept you down an' you had to
wurk, now I can't wurk, an' I am still down. Not allowed
to wurk an' still down. Its all hard, slavery and
freedom, both bad when you can't eat. The ole bees makes
de honey comb, the young bee makes de honey, niggers
makes de cotton an' corn an' de white folks gets de money.
Dis wus de case in Slavery time an' its de case now. De
nigger do mos' de hard wurk on de farms now, and de white
folks still git de money dat de nigger's labor makes."

LE

STATE EDITORIAL IDENTIFICATION FORM

STATE: North Carolina

RECEIVED FROM: (State office) Asheville

MS. Interview with W.L.Bost   WORDS 2,000   QUOTA
    Ex-slave.
STATE GUIDE_____LOCAL GUIDE_____NON-GUIDE X

TABLE OF CONTENTS DIVISION_____

COMPLETE FOR THIS SECTION?_____WHAT PERCENTAGE REMAINS?_____

PREFINAL REVISE NO._____WASHINGTON CRITICISM_____

PREFINAL REVISE NO._____WASHINGTON CRITICISM_____

PREFINAL REVISE NO._____WASHINGTON CRITICISM_____

PREFINAL REVISE NO._____WASHINGTON CIRITCISM_____

PREFINAL NEW: _____

VOLUNTEER CONSULTANT: Name _____

                        Position _____

                        Address _____

                        _____

                        By_____

                        Position_____

DATE: Sept.27, 1937.

My Massa's name was Jonas Bost. He had a hotel in Newton, North Carolina. My mother and grandmother both belonged to the Bost family. My ole Massa had two large plantations one about three miles from Newton and another four miles away. It took a lot of niggers to keep the work a goin' on them both. The women folks had to work in the hotel and in the big house in town. Ole Missus she was a good woman. She never allowed the Massa to buy or sell any slaves. There never was an overseer on the whole plantation. The oldest colored man always looked after the niggers. We niggers lived better than the niggers on the other plantations.

Lord child, I remember when I was a little boy, 'bout ten years, the speculators come through Newton with droves of slaves. They always stay at our place. The poor critters nearly froze to death. They always come 'long on the last of December so that the niggers would be ready for sale on the first day of January. Many the time I see four or five of them chained together. They never had enough clothes on to keep a cat warm. The women never wore anything but a thin dress and a petticoat and one underwear. I've seen the ice balls hangin' on to the bottom of their dresses as they ran along, jes like sheep in a pasture 'fore they are sheared. They never wore any shoes. Jes

run along on the ground, all spewed up with ice. The speculators always rode on horses and drove the pore niggers.
When they get cold, they make 'em run 'til they are warm
again.

The speculators stayed in the hotel and put the niggers
in the quarters jes like droves of hogs. All through the
night I could hear them mournin' and prayin'. I didn't
know the Lord would let people live who were so cruel. The
gates were always locked and they was a guard on the outside
to shoot anyone who tried to run away. Lord miss, them
slaves look jes like droves of turkeys runnin' along in
front of them horses.

I remember when they put 'em on the block to sell 'em.
The ones 'tween 18 and 30 always bring the most money. The
auctioneer he stand off at a distance and cry 'em off as
they stand on the block. I can hear his voice as long as
I live.

If the one they going to sell was a young Negro man this
is what he say: "Now gentlemen and fellow-citizens here is
a big black buck Negro. He's stout as a mule. Good for
any kin' o'work an' he never gives any trouble. How much
am I offered for him?" And then the sale would commence,
and the nigger would be sold to the highest bidder.

If they put up a young nigger woman the auctioneer cry
out: "Here's a young nigger wench, how much am I offered

for her?" The pore thing stand on the block a shiverin'
an' a shakin' nearly froze to death. When they sold many
of the pore mothers beg the speculators to sell 'em with
their husbands, but the speculator only take what he want.
So maybe the pore thing never see her husban' agin.

Ole' Massa always see that we get plenty to eat. O' course
it was no fancy rashions. Jes corn bread, milk, fat meat,
and 'lasses but the Lord knows that was lots more than other
pore niggers got. Some of them had such bad masters.

Us pore niggers never 'lowed to learn anything. All the
readin' they ever hear was when they/carried through the
big Bible. The Massa say that keep the slaves in they places.
They was one nigger boy in Newton who was terrible smart.
He learn to read an' write. He take other colored children
out in the fields and teach 'em about the Bible, but they
forgit it 'fore the nex' Sunday.

Then the paddyrollers they keep close watch on the pore
niggers so they have no chance to do anything or go anywhere.
They jes' like policemen, only worser. 'Cause they never
let the niggers go anywhere without a pass from his master.
If you wasn't in your proper place when the paddyrollers
come they lash you til' you was black and blue. The women
got 15 lashes and the men 30. That is for jes bein' out
without a pass. If the nigger done anything worse he was
taken to the jail and put in the whippin' post. They was

two holes cut for the arms stretch up in the air and a block
to put your feet in, then they whip you with cowhide whip .
An' the clothes shore never get any of them licks.

I remember how they kill one nigger whippin' him with
the bull whip. Many the pore nigger nearly killed with the
bull whip. But this one die. He was a stubborn Negro and
didn't do as much work as his Massa thought he ought to. He
been lashed lot before. So they take him to the whippin'
post, and then they strip his clothes off and then the man
stan' off and cut him with the whip. His back was cut all
to pieces. The cuts about half inch apart. Then after they
whip him they tie him down and put salt on him. Then after
he lie in the sun awhile they whip him agin. But when they
finish with him he was dead.

Plenty of the colored women have children by the white men.
She know better than to not do what he say. Didn't have much
of that until the men from South Carolina come up here and
settle and bring slaves. Then they take them very same
children what have they own blood and make slaves out of
them. If the Missus find out she raise revolution. But
she hardly find out. The white men not going to tell and
the nigger women were always afraid to. So they jes go on
hopin' that thing won't be that way always.

I remember how the driver, he was the man who did most of

the whippin', use to whip some of the niggers. He would tie
their hands together and then put their hands down over their
knees, then take a stick and stick it 'tween they hands and
knees. Then when he take hold of them and beat 'em first
on one side then on the other.

Us niggers never have chance to go to Sunday School and
church. The white folks feared for niggers to get any religion and education, but I reckon somethin' inside jes told
us about God and that there was a better place hereafter. We
would sneak off and have prayer meetin'. Sometimes the
paddyrollers catch us and beat us good but that didn't keep
us from tryin'. I remember one old song we use to sing when
we meet down in the woods back of the barn. My mother she
sing an' pray to the Lord to deliver us out o' slavery. She
always say she thankful she was never sold from her children,
and that our Massa not so mean as some of the others. But
the old song it went something like this:

"Oh, mother lets go down, lets go down, lets go down,
lets go down.

Oh, mother lets go down, down in the valley to pray.

As I went down in the valley to pray

Studyin' about that good ole way

Who shall wear that starry crown.

Good Lord show me the way."

Then the other part was just like that except it said 'father' instead of 'mother', and then 'sister' and then 'brother'.

Then they sing sometime:

"We camp a while in the wilderness, in the wilderness,
in the wilderness.

We camp a while in the wilderness, where the Lord makes
me happy

And then I'm a goin' home!"

I don't remember much about the war. There was no fightin'
done in Newton. Jes a skirmish or two. Most of the people get
everything jes ready to run when the Yankee sojers come through
the town. This was toward the las' of the war. Cose the niggers
knew what all the fightin' was about, but they didn't dare say
anything. The man who owned the slaves was too mad as it was,
and if the niggers say anything they get shot right then and
thar. The sojers tell us after the war that we get food,
clothes, and wages from our Massas else we leave. But they
was very few that ever got anything. Our ole Massa say he
not gwine pay us anything, corse his money was no good, but
he wouldn't pay us if it had been.

Then the Ku Klux Klan come 'long. They were terrible danger-
ous. They wear long gowns, touch the ground. They ride horses
through the town at night and if they find a Negro that tries to
get nervy or have a little bit for himself, they lash him nearly
to death and gag him and leave him to do the bes' he can. Some
time they put sticks in the top of the tall thing they wear and
then put an extra head up there with scary eyes and great big

mouth, then they stick it clear up in the air to scare the poor Negroes to death.

They had another thing they call the 'Donkey Devil' that was jes as bad. They take the skin of a donkey and get inside of it and run after the pore Negroes. Oh, Miss them was bad times, them was bad times. I know folks think the books tell the truth, but they shore don't. Us pore niggers had to take it all.

Then after the war was over we was afraid to move. Jes like tarpins or turtles after 'mancipation. Jes stick our heads out to see how the land lay. My mammy stay with Marse Jonah for 'bout a year after freedom then ole Solomon Hall made her an offer. Ole man Hall was a good man if there ever was one. He freed all of his slaves about two years 'fore 'mancipation and gave each of them so much money when he died, that is he put that in his will. But when he die his sons and daughters never give anything to the pore Negroes. My mother went to live on the place belongin' to the nephew of Solomon Hall. All of her six children went with her. Mother she cook for the white folks an' the children make crop. When the first year was up us children got the first money we had in our lives. My mother certainly was happy.

We live on this place for over four years. When I was 'bout twenty year old I married a girl from West Virginia but she didn't live but jes 'bout a year. I stayed down there for a

year or so and then I met Mamie. We came here and both of us
went to work, we work at the same place. We bought this little
piece of ground 'bout forty-two years ago. We gave $125. for
it. We had to buy the lumber to build the house a little at
a time but finally we got the house done. Its been a good
home for us and the children. We have two daughters and one
adopted son. Both of the girls are good cooks. One of them
lives in New Jersey and cooks in a big hotel. She and her
husband come to see us about once a year. The other one is
in Philadelphia. They both have plenty. But the adopted boy,
he was part white. We took him when he was a small and did the
best we could by him. He never did like to 'sociate with colored
people. I remember one time when he was a small child I took
him to town and the conductor made me put him in the front of
the street car cause he thought I was just caring for him and
that he was a white boy. Well, we sent him to school until he
finished. Then he joined the navy. I ain't seem him in several
years. The last letter I got from him he say he ain't spoke to
a colored/since he has been there. This made me mad so I took
his insurance policy and cashed it. I didn't want nothin' to
do with him, if he deny his own color.

Very few of the Negroes ever get anywhere; they never have
no education. I knew one Negro who got to be a policeman in
Salisbury once and he was a good one too. When my next birth-
day comes in December I will be eighty-eight years old. That
is if the Lord lets me live and I shore hope He does.

N. C. District No.___3_____   Subject___Mary Wallace Bowe___

Worker___Travis Jordan_____   ___Ex-slave 81 Years_____

Durham County Home

Durham, N.C.

MARY WALLACE BOWE

Ex-slave 81 years

My name is Mary Wallace Bowe. I ~~wuz~~ *was* nine years ole at de surrender.

My mammy an' pappy, Susan an' Lillman Graves, ~~fus'~~ *first* belonged to Marse Fountain an' Mis' Fanny Tu'berville, but Marse Fountain sold me, my mammy an' my brother George to Mis' Fanny's sister, Mis' Virginia Graves. Mis' Virginia's husban' ~~wuz~~ *was* Marse Docter Graves. Dey lived on de ole Elijah Graves estate not far from Marse Fountain's plantation here in Durham county, an' Mis' Virginia an' Mis' Fanny seed each other near 'bout every day.

I ~~wuz~~ *was* little when Marse Fountain an' Marse Doctor went to de war but I remembers it. I remembers it kaze Mis' Fanny stood on de po'ch smilin' an' wavin' at Marse Fountain ~~'twell~~ *'til* he went 'roun' de curve in de road, den she fell to de floor like she ~~wuz~~ *was* dead. I thought she ~~wuz~~ *was* dead ~~'twell~~ *'till* Mis' Virginia th'owed some water in her face an' she opened her eyes.

De nex' day Mis' Virginia took me an' mammy an' we all went over an' stayed wid Mis' Fanny kaze she ~~wuz~~ *was* skeered, an' so dey'd be company for each other. Mammy waited on Mis' Virginia an' he'ped Surella Tu'berville, Mis' Fanny's house girl, sweep an' make up de beds an' things. I ~~wuz~~ *was* little but mammy made me work. I shook de rugs, brung in de kindlin' an run 'roun' waitin' on Mis' Virginia an' Mis' Fanny, ~~such as~~ *doin' things like* totin' dey basket of keys, bringin' dey shawls an' such as dat. Dey ~~wuz~~ *was* all de time ~~talkin~~ *talki* 'bout de folks fightin' an' what dey would do if de Yankees come.

Every time dey _talk_ ~~tawk~~ Mis' Fanny set an' twist her han's an' say:
"What is we gwine do, Sister, what is we gwine do?"

Mis' Virginia try to pacify Mis' Fanny. She say, 'Don' yo'
worry none, Honey, I'll fix dem Yankees when dey come.' Den she
set her mouf. When she done dat I run an' hid behin' Mis' Fanny's
chair kaze I done seed Mis' Virginia set her mouf befo' an' I
knowed she meant biznes'.

I didn' have sense _enough_ ~~enuff~~ to be skeered den kaze I hadn'
never seed no Yankee sojers, but _'twaren't_ ~~twon'~~ long befo' I wuz skeered.
De Yankees come one _mornin'_ ~~mawnin'~~, an' dey ripped, Oh, Lawd, how dey
did rip. When dey rode up to de gate an' come stompin' to de
house, Mis' Fanny 'gun to cry. 'Tell dem somethin', Sister, tell
dem somethin', she tole Mis' Virginia.

Mis' Virginia she ain' done no cryin'. When she seed dem
Yankees comin' 'cross de hill, she run 'roun' an' got all de
jewelry. She took off de rings an' pins she an' Mis' Fanny had
on an' she got all de things out of de jewelry box an' give dem to
pappy. "Hide dem, Lillman" she tole pappy, "hide dem some place
whare dem thieves won't fin' dem".

Pappy had on high top boots. He didn' do nothin but stuff
all dat jewelry right down in dem boots, den he strutted all 'roun'
dem Yankees laughin' to heself. _O_ dey cussed when dey couldn'
fin' no jewelry a tall. Dey didn' fin' no silver neither kaze us
niggers done he'p Mis' Fanny an' Mis' Virginia hide dat. We
done toted it all down to de cottin gin house an' hid it in de

loose cotton piled on de floor. When dey couldn' fin' nothin'
er big sojer went up to Mis' Virginia who wuz standin' in de hall.
He look at her an' say: 'Yo's skeered of me, ain' yo'?'

Mis' Virginia ain' batted no eye yet. She tole him, "If I
wuz gwine to be skeered, I'd be skeered of somethin'. I sho ain'
of no ugly, braggin' Yankee."

De man tu'ned red an he say: "If you don' tell me where you
done hide dat silver I'se gwine to make you skeered."

Mis' Virginia's chin went up higher. She set her mouf an'
look at dat sojer twell he drap his eyes, Den she tole him dat
some folks done come an' got de silver, dat dey done toted it off.
She didn' tell him dat it wuz us niggers dat done toted it down
to de cotton gin house.

In dem days dey wuz peddlers gwine 'roun' do country sellin'
things. Dey toted big packs on dey backs filled wid everythin'
from needles an' thimbles to bed spreads an'fryin' pans. One day
er peddlar stopped at Mis' Fanny's house. He wuz de uglies' man
I ever seed. He wuz tall an' bony wid black whiskers an' black
bushy hair an' curious eyes dat set way back in his head. Dey
wuz dark an' look like er dog's eyes after you done hit him. He
set down on de po'ch an' opened his pack, an' it wuz so hot an'
he looked so tired, dat Mis' Fanny give him er cool drink of milk
dat done been settin' in de spring house. All de time Mis' Fanny
wuz lookin' at de things in de pack an' buyin', de man kept up er
runnin' talk He ask her how many niggers dey had; how many men

dey had fightin' on de 'Federate side, an' what *was* she gwine do
if de niggers *was* set free. Den he *ask* her if she knowed Mistah
Abraham Lincoln.

'Bout dat time Mis' Virginia come to de door an' heard what
he said. She blaze up like *a* lightwood fire an' *told* dat peddlar
dat dey didn't want to know nothin' 'bout Mistah Lincoln; dat dey
knowed too much already, an' dat his name *wasn't* 'lowed called in
her house. Den she say he *wasn't* nothin' but *a* black debil messin'
in other folks *business*, an' dat she'd shoot him on sight if she
had half *a* chance.

De man laughed. "Maybe *Mr. Lincoln* ain't so bad," he told her. Den
he packed his pack an' went off down de road, an' Mis' Virginia
watched him *'till* he went out of sight 'roun' de bend.

Two or three weeks later Mis' Fanny got *a* letter. De
letter *was* from dat peddlar. He tole her dat he *was* Abraham
Lincoln hese'f; dat he wuz peddlin' over de country as *a* spy, an'
he thanked her for de res' on her shady po'ch an' de cool glass
of milk she give him.

When dat letter come Mis' Virginia got so hoppin' mad dat
she took all de stuff Mis' Fanny done bought from Mistah Lincoln
an' made us niggers burn it on de ash pile. Den she made pappy
rake up de ashes an' th'ow dem in de creek.

N. C. District No. 2   Subject Ex-Slave Recollections

Worker Mary A. Hicks   Person Interviewed Lucy Brown

No. Words 577   Editor Daisy Bailey Waitt

EX-SLAVE RECOLLECTIONS

An interview with Lucy Brown of Hecktown, Durham, Durham
County, May 20, 1937. She does not know her age.

"I wuz jist a little thing when de war wuz over an'
I doan 'member much ter tell yo'. Mostly what I does
know I hyard my mammy tell it.

"We belonged to John Neal of Person County. I doan
know who my pappy wuz, but my mammy wuz named Rosseta
an' her mammy's name 'fore her wuz Rosseta. I had one
sister named Jenny an' one brother named Ben.

"De marster wuz good ter us, in a way, but he ain't
'lowin' no kinds of frolickin' so when we had a meetin'
we had ter do it secret. We'd turn down a wash pot outside de do', an' dat would ketch de fuss so marster
neber knowed nothin' 'bout hit.

"On Sundays we went ter church at de same place de
white folkses did. De white folkses rid an' de niggers
walked, but eben do' we wored wooden bottomed shoes we wuz
proud an' mostly happy. We had good clothes an' food an'
not much abuse. I doan know de number of slaves, I wuz
so little.

"My mammy said dat slavery wuz a whole lot wuser 'fore
I could 'member. She tol' me how some of de slaves had

dere babies in de fiel's lak de cows done, an' she said
dat 'fore de babies wuz borned dey tied de mammy down
on her face if'en dey had ter whup her ter keep from
ruinin' de baby.

"She said dat dar wuz ghostes an' some witches back
den, but I doan know nothin' 'bout dem things.

"Naw, I can't tell yo' my age but I will tell yo'
dat eber'body what lives in dis block am either my chile
or gran'chile. I can't tell yo' prexackly how many dar
is o' 'em, but I will tell you dat my younges' chile's
baby am fourteen years old, an' dat she's got fourteen
youngin's, one a year jist lak I had till I had sixteen.

"I'se belonged ter de church since I wuz a baby an'
I tells dem eber'day dat dey shore will miss me when I'se
gone."

N.C. District No. 2

No. Words: 462

Mary Hicks: Worker

Subject: PLANTATION LIFE IN GEORGIA.

Reference: Midge Burnett

Editor: George L. Andrews

PLANTATION LIFE IN GEORGIA

An interview with Midge Burnett, 80 years old, of 1300 S.
Bloodworth Street, Raleigh, North Carolina.

"I wus borned in Georgia eighty years ago, de son
of Jim an' Henretta Burnett an' de slave of Marse William
Joyner.

"I wurked on de farm durin' slavery times, among de
cotton, corn, an' sugar cane. De wurk wusn't so hard an' we
had plenty of time ter have fun an' ter git inter meanness,
dat's why Marse William had ter have so many patterollers
on de place.

"Marse William had near three hundret slaves an' he
kept seben patterollers ter keep things goin' eben. De slaves
ain't run away. Naw sir, dey ain't, dey knows good things
when dey sees dem an' dey ain't leavin' dem nother. De only
trouble wus dat dey wus crazy 'bout good times an' dey'd
shoot craps er bust.

"De patterollers 'ud watch all de paths leadin' frum de
plantation an' when dey ketched a nigger leavin' dey whupped
him an' run him home. As I said de patterollers watched all
paths, but dar wus a number of little paths what run through
de woods dat nobody ain't watched case dey ain't knowed dat
de paths wus dar.

"On moonlight nights yo' could hear a heap of voices an' when yo' peep ober de dike dar am a gang of niggers a-shootin' craps an' bettin' eber'thing dey has stold frum de plantation. Sometimes a pretty yaller gal er a fat black gal would be dar, but mostly hit would be jist men.

"Dar wus a ribber nearby de plantation an' we niggers swum dar ever' Sadday an' we fished dar a heap too. We ketched a big mess of fish ever' week an' dese come in good an' helped ter save rations ter boot. Dat's what Marse William said, an' he believed in havin' a good time too.

"We had square dances dat las' all night on holidays an' we had a Christmas tree an' a Easter egg hunt an' all dat, case Marse William intended ter make us a civilized bunch of blacks.

"Marse William ain't eber hit one of us a single lick till de day when we heard dat de Yankees wus a-comin'. One big nigger jumps up an' squalls, 'Lawd bless de Yankees'.

"Marse yells back, 'God damn de Yankees', an' he slaps big Mose a sumerset right outen de do'. Nobody else wanted ter git slapped soe ever'body got outen dar in a hurry an' nobody else dasen't say Yankees ter de marster.

"Eben when somebody seed de Yankees comin' Mose wont go tell de marster 'bout hit, but when Marster William wus hilt tight twixt two of dem big husky Yankees he cussed 'em

as hard as he can. Dey carries him off an' dey put him in de
jail at Atlanta an' dey keeps him fer a long time.

"Atter de surrender we left dar an' we moves ter Star,
South Carolina, whar I still wurks 'roun' on de farm. I
stayed on dar till fifty years ago when I married Roberta
Thomas an' we moved ter Raleigh. We have five chilluns an'
we's moughty proud of 'em, but since I had de stroke we has
been farin' bad, an' I'se hopin' ter git my ole aged
pension."

EH

TITLES IN THE

SLAVE NARRATIVES SERIES

FROM APPLEWOOD BOOKS

ALABAMA SLAVE NARRATIVES
ISBN 1-55709-010-6 • $14.95
Paperback • 7-1/2" x 9-1/4" • 168 pp

ARKANSAS SLAVE NARRATIVES
ISBN 1-55709-011-4 • $14.95
Paperback • 7-1/2" x 9-1/4" • 172 pp

FLORIDA SLAVE NARRATIVES
ISBN 1-55709-012-2 • $14.95
Paperback • 7-1/2" x 9-1/4" • 168 pp

GEORGIA SLAVE NARRATIVES
ISBN 1-55709-013-0 • $14.95
Paperback • 7-1/2" x 9-1/4" • 172 pp

INDIANA SLAVE NARRATIVES
ISBN 1-55709-014-9 • $14.95
Paperback • 7-1/2" x 9-1/4" • 140 pp

KENTUCKY SLAVE NARRATIVES
ISBN 1-55709-016-5 • $14.95
Paperback • 7-1/2" x 9-1/4" • 136 pp

MARYLAND SLAVE NARRATIVES
ISBN 1-55709-017-3 • $14.95
Paperback • 7-1/2" x 9-1/4" • 88 pp

MISSISSIPPI SLAVE NARRATIVES
ISBN 1-55709-018-1 • $14.95
Paperback • 7-1/2" x 9-1/4" • 184 pp

MISSOURI SLAVE NARRATIVES
ISBN 1-55709-019-X • $14.95
Paperback • 7-1/2" x 9-1/4" • 172 pp

NORTH CAROLINA SLAVE NARRATIVES
ISBN 1-55709-020-3 • $14.95
Paperback • 7-1/2" x 9-1/4" • 168 pp

OHIO SLAVE NARRATIVES
ISBN 1-55709-021-1 • $14.95
Paperback • 7-1/2" x 9-1/4" • 128 pp

OKLAHOMA SLAVE NARRATIVES
ISBN 1-55709-022-X • $14.95
Paperback • 7-1/2" x 9-1/4" • 172 pp

SOUTH CAROLINA SLAVE NARRATIVES
1-55709-023-8 • $14.95
Paperback • 7-1/2" x 9-1/4" • 172 pp

TENNESSEE SLAVE NARRATIVES
ISBN 1-55709-024-6 • $14.95
Paperback • 7-1/2" x 9-1/4" • 92 pp

VIRGINIA SLAVE NARRATIVES
ISBN 1-55709-025-4 • $14.95
Paperback • 7-1/2" x 9-1/4" • 68 pp

* * * * * * * * * * * * * * *

IN THEIR VOICES: SLAVE NARRATIVES
A companion CD of original recordings
made by the Federal Writers' Project.
Former slaves from many states tell
stories, sing long-remembered songs,
and recall the era of American slavery.
This invaluable treasure trove of oral
history, through the power of voices of
those now gone, brings back to life the
people who lived in slavery.
ISBN 1-55709-026-2 • $19.95
Audio CD

* * * * * * * * * * * * * * *

TO ORDER, CALL 800-277-5312 OR
VISIT US ON THE WEB AT WWW.AWB.COM

LaVergne, TN USA
11 April 2011
223805LV00004B/40/A